"I was pregnant with your son, not Charles's."

Dillon shook his head to clear his mind and his ears. "My son?"

Monique nodded and nervously ran her hand through her hair. He wondered if it was as soft as he remembered. Stupid thought, given what she'd just told him, but a much easier thought to entertain than the news that she'd given his son to another man. He looked at this woman he'd loved with all his heart and wondered if he'd ever really known her. "Why should I believe you?"

"Why should I lie?"

"Why *did* you lie?" he returned.

ANGELA BENSON

Second Chance Dad

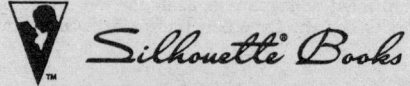

Published by Silhouette Books
America's Publisher of Contemporary Romance

If you purchased this book without a cover you should be aware that this book is stolen property. It was reported as "unsold and destroyed" to the publisher, and neither the author nor the publisher has received any payment for this "stripped book."

 SILHOUETTE BOOKS

ISBN 0-373-28549-3

SECOND CHANCE DAD

Copyright © 1997 by Angela D. Benson

All rights reserved. Except for use in any review, the reproduction or utilization of this work in whole or in part in any form by any electronic, mechanical or other means, now known or hereafter invented, including xerography, photocopying and recording, or in any information storage or retrieval system, is forbidden without the written permission of the editorial office, Silhouette Books, 233 Broadway, New York, NY 10279 U.S.A.

All characters in this book have no existence outside the imagination of the author and have no relation whatsoever to anyone bearing the same name or names. They are not even distantly inspired by any individual known or unknown to the author, and all incidents are pure invention.

This edition published by arrangement with Harlequin Books S.A.

® and TM are trademarks of Harlequin Books S.A., used under license. Trademarks indicated with ® are registered in the United States Patent and Trademark Office, the Canadian Trade Marks Office and in other countries.

Visit Silhouette Books at www.eHarlequin.com

Printed in U.S.A.

Books by Angela Benson

Silhouette Special Edition

A Family Wedding #1085
Second Chance Dad #1146

ANGELA BENSON

sold her first book in 1993 and it was a dream come true. Since then, she has continued to dream and she's still seeing those dreams come true.

A graduate of Spellman College and Georgia Tech in Atlanta, Angela is a former engineer who now writes full-time. She was born and raised in Alabama and currently divides her time between her home in the Atlanta suburbs and her home-away-from-home in the college town of Athens, Georgia. When she's not weaving her own tales of romance, Angela can be found curled up on her couch reading her favorite romance authors.

Chapter One

Monique stood on the cracked concrete sidewalk in front of the faded brick two-story building. Its massive white columns and imposing cement steps loomed before her petite, five-foot-four-inch frame, making her feel as small and as insignificant as she'd felt ten years ago. Good ol' Elberton High School, she thought, shaking her head. It still looks the same after all these years.

Her heart picked up a rhythm from the past and her lips curved in a smile as heavily hooded dark eyes and a contrasting wide, white-tooth smile set in a caramel-colored masculine face flashed in her mind. Dillon Bell. The first man she'd ever loved.

Her smile faltered as another image of that same face replaced the first one. The eyes in this face were wide and brimmed with tears that she'd never before seen there. The smile was absent, replaced by a grimace, and the tightness to his features told her he was in pain.

She reached in the pocket of her white walking shorts for a tissue, then wiped at the tears that filled her own eyes. She knew she couldn't change the past, couldn't take back the awful words she'd spoken, but she could try to make amends. She could make right the biggest wrong she'd ever committed.

She stuffed the tissue back in her pocket and, in an attempt to shake off the negative spirit that wanted to settle around her, took confident steps toward the entrance of the school. As she climbed the last step, the steel doors opened.

"Come on, Calvin."

Her skin tingled at the sound of the rich, baritone voice that had often whispered words of love and family in her teenage ears.

"Okay, Daddy," a small voice answered.

His son, she knew. His *other* son. Monique held her breath and waited for Dillon and his son to exit the building, refusing to give in to the fear that told her to run, to wait for a better time to see him again.

"Ready to go?" she heard Dillon ask.

No answer came, but a young boy dressed in white sneakers and socks, a blue golf shirt and khaki shorts, stepped outside. The youngster, whom she guessed to be about four, saw her and stared, obviously surprised by her presence.

Dillon backed into his son as he was locking the door, causing the boy to turn away from her for a brief second and giving her a private moment to compose herself. The boy looked so much like Glenn had at that age. They could be...

"There's a lady out here, Daddy," came the child's

voice, which stopped her thoughts. "She's pretty." He turned back around and smiled at her, his surprise at seeing her replaced with what she thought was acceptance.

"A pretty lady, huh?" Dillon repeated, giving the door handle a final shake to assure that it was secured. He turned around and opened his mouth to speak, but before he could form his words, his dark brown eyes met hers. She knew he'd been transported ten years back in time just as she had been. She saw warmth spread across his face at the memories, and then she saw that warmth quickly replaced by caution. She swallowed her hurt, telling herself that his response was no less than she expected. No less than she deserved.

"Hi, Dillon," she said, praying her voice didn't falter, praying he didn't still hate her.

"Hi" was all he said, but the words he didn't say rang in her ears and kept her eyes glued to his.

She watched him and he watched her as the silence between them stretched as if to envelop the distance between them. Her first thought was that he and his son were dressed in matching outfits. Her second thought was that he'd gotten more attractive. His shoulders were wider and his chest more defined. He was now the man in body that he'd always been in soul. Her glance slid to his hands. Large, vanilla-wafer-shaded brown hands. Hands that had comforted her, teased her and loved her. It hit her suddenly how much she missed those hands.

Monique took a deep breath and let her gaze travel back to his strong, but now-shuttered face. Their eyes met and held, but neither spoke.

"Hi." The boy's voice sounded, interrupting the

safety of the silence. "I'm Calvin. What's your name?"

Monique dragged her glance from Dillon's dark eyes to the identical ones in Calvin's face. "I'm Monique Morgan," she said, bending down and extending her hand to the tot. "I went to school with your dad." She glanced up at Dillon and gave him a slight smile, before looking back down at the little boy. "A very long time ago."

"Do you know my mama?"

Monique shook her head, but before she could speak, Dillon's voice filled the air.

"No, your mother and I went to college together. Monique and I went to high school together right here at Elberton High."

Calvin turned to Monique, his eyes wide. "You did?" He scrunched up his nose. "How old are you?"

The sincerity of the question made Monique and Dillon laugh. It was a good laugh, too. When it ended, some of the tension between them was gone.

Dillon rubbed his hand across his son's head. "Never ask a lady her age, son. They don't like that."

"Why?"

Monique anticipated the question before Calvin asked it. Glenn still asked his share of "why" questions. "Because women don't like to tell their ages, that's why," she said.

The boy shook his head, clearly not understanding women. "I'm four," he said, lifting four stubby fingers on his right hand as if offering to swap information with her.

Monique tweaked his flat nose. "I'm still not telling."

The boy laughed and the sound made her insides curl up and relax. She looked up and saw Dillon observing his son with a pleased, but surprised expression on his face. "He's a wonderful boy, Dillon. So much like you."

Dillon nodded, then dropped an arm around his son's shoulders in a loving and protective gesture. "Thank you, I think," he said with a lift of his brow. "Listen, we're going for ice cream. Would you like to go with us?"

Dillon mentally chastised himself as the threesome strolled to the ice-cream shop. He'd wanted to recall his invitation as soon as it had passed his lips. He didn't want ice cream with Monique now or ever. From the moment he learned she was returning to Elberton to work at the high school where he was vice principal, he'd gone over several scenarios for handling their first meeting. None of them included inviting her for ice cream.

He cut his glance to his left and saw that her lips were curved in a smile as she listened intently to Calvin telling her about his outing today. She nodded her head in a way that was familiar to him. It was a parent's nod that said she shared the boy's excitement even though she didn't quite understand what he was talking about.

"Daddy says I can go to the high school when I'm bigger," Calvin informed Monique with pride. He turned his head toward Dillon, who'd shortened his stride so that his son could keep pace during the short walk from the high school to the ice-cream shop. "You said that, didn't you, Daddy?"

Dillon smiled the joy that he felt. His son's happiness was most important to him. And today Calvin was happy. His animated voice made that clear. "Sure did, sport."

Calvin turned back to Monique. "Told you," he said. Then with an ease and trust that only a child could muster, he slipped one of his small hands into one of Monique's.

Dillon checked her face for her response to his son's familiarity, and the wide, open smile he saw there tugged at the closed door of his heart. "I believe you," she said to Calvin. "The way you're growing, you'll be a big boy in no time at all."

Calvin beamed. Dillon could think of no other word to describe the joy expressed on his son's often-somber face. He glanced again at the smiling Monique and the door to his heart gave a little.

While his son continued his recitation to Monique, Dillon directed his attention to topics that Calvin wouldn't be thinking about for years. Facing straight ahead, he used his peripheral vision to explore the womanly body he'd once known so well. The years had only brought good changes in Monique. Her chin-length hair was no longer curly, but straight, and lay in soft waves about her still-innocent-looking face. She'd probably gained five pounds, and if his memory served him right, those pounds had been added to her legs and chest. Not as fat, though. No, the strong, brown legs extending from her white walking shorts hinted at lean hips. His eyes moved to her chest, where her sunglasses rested between her breasts on the thin material of her pink tank top. She definitely had more cleavage now than she'd had back then. He remembered her lamenting her less-than-ample breasts. He'd always thought her handful enough, though he admitted the extra pounds looked good in the skimpy top.

When they reached the blue stucco-faced building that housed the ice-cream shop, Dillon stepped ahead of Monique and Calvin, then past the slide and swings the shop owner provided for the kids, and opened the door. Monique allowed Calvin to enter first and Dillon followed behind her. Naturally, his eyes took in the delightful sway of her hips as she walked with Calvin to the counter, the child's favorite place to have ice cream.

Monique helped Calvin climb up on a white, wooden stool, then she took the one next to him. Dillon walked around and took the stool on the other side of his son. He told himself that he wasn't using Calvin as a barrier to keep from getting close to Monique.

When the attendant approached them, Calvin quickly ordered his favorite, strawberry ice cream. Dillon expected Monique to order her favorite, black cherry, but she surprised him by choosing strawberry, as well. He guessed her taste in ice cream had changed over the years, and he briefly speculated what else had. When he ordered his usual chocolate, she smiled at him and he wondered if she remembered chocolate was his favorite. He didn't ask, though, because Calvin dominated her attention. His son was definitely taken with Monique. The boy barely paused to breathe between sentences as he chattered away.

Dillon smiled when Calvin stopped talking to eat his ice cream. Apparently, Monique's charm couldn't compete with the taste of his son's favorite treat. Monique met his smile over Calvin's head and he guessed she was thinking the same thing. The shared smile reminded him of the old days when they'd often finished each other's sentences or spoken each other's thoughts or smiled at some private joke. It had always been that way with them. Almost as if they were one person. Until the night of the senior prom. The door to his heart slammed shut at the memory.

"Calvin," a child's voice called from behind them.

Dillon turned and saw one of the kids from Calvin's day care. Finished with his ice cream in record time, Calvin quickly scrambled down from his stool. His little friend whispered something in his ear, then Calvin turned and asked, "Can we go play on the slide?"

"Sure." Dillon wagged a finger at both boys. "But no pushing. Remember what happened last time."

Calvin dashed off with his friend after a mere nod of understanding.

"What happened last time?" Monique asked.

Dillon pushed his ice-cream dish away from him and rested his elbows on the counter. "Let's just say boys can get rowdy sometimes—even a tyke as reserved as Calvin."

Monique's brown eyes widened and he thought, as he'd always thought, that her coloring was perfect. Honey brown hair, chestnut brown eyes and doughnut brown skin. Too bad beauty was only skin-deep.

"Reserved? He doesn't seem reserved to me."

Dillon shrugged. "So I noticed. He doesn't usually take to people the way he's taken to you."

"I hope that means he likes me." A light formed in her eyes that matched the wistfulness of her words. He could almost believe Calvin's friendship meant something to her. Almost.

"He likes you, all right," Dillon said. "But then, children are not known for being the best judges of character."

The light in those big brown eyes dimmed and he felt like an idiot for his attack. "Whatever I've done, Dillon," she said, "I've never mistreated a child. I hope Calvin likes me because he senses that I'm a nice person."

"Look, Monique, I'm sorry I said that." He instinctively touched her hand, a comforting gesture at odds with his need to hurt her as she'd once hurt him. The feel of her satiny skin sent shock waves through him and he snatched his hand back.

She looked down to where his hand had touched hers. "You have every right to think badly of me, Dillon. I treated you miserably ten years ago."

He shrugged his broad shoulders as if it didn't matter. As if it still didn't hurt. But it did. "That was ten years ago. Water under the bridge, as they say. There's no need to go back there. You married a man you loved, and later I married a woman I loved. I have a son I love, and you have a child you love. I don't have any regrets. Do you?"

She stared at her empty bowl, the melted ice cream symbolic of her relationship with Dillon. It, too, had once been solid and so very good. Now it was nothing but a soggy mess. She looked back up at him. "There are some things I regret," she answered honestly.

"Take some advice from the master. Don't look back. What's done is done and it can't be undone. Just try to make the best of every day."

"Speaking from experience?" she asked.

He slid off his stool and stood up. "It's the best teacher in the world," he said, a weak smile tugging at the corners of his mouth. He threw a couple of bills on the counter. "The ice cream's on me. Welcome back, Monique." He turned and walked toward the outdoor playground.

"So Monique's back," Dillon's younger brother, Donald, said to nobody in particular. The Bell family had just finished Sunday dinner and Donald, Dillon and their mother sat in the family room of the house where Dillon had grown up. Donald flipped TV channels using the remote while Dillon read the Sunday paper and his mother clipped coupons.

"Melissa Williams's mother saw you two in the ice-cream shop with Calvin," his mother added, not looking up from her coupons. "Do you think that was wise, son?" Her tone said she didn't think it was.

"What's wrong with Dillon having some ice cream with his old girlfriend?" Donald asked after another click of the remote. He gave Dillon a wink and a grin. "Unless he's planning on making her his new girlfriend. Calvin sure seemed taken with her. He couldn't talk about anything but his 'Moni' at dinner."

Dillon wished Calvin were here right now, instead of out with his grandfather on their usual Sunday after-dinner walk around the block.

"You have to watch that, Dillon." His mother rested her scissors on the stack of coupons in her lap. "You can't afford to let Calvin get attached to people who aren't going to be permanent in his life."

Dillon had firsthand experience with getting attached to the wrong people. He thought he'd played it safe after Monique, but Teena, his ex-wife, had gotten to him through Calvin. How could a mother desert her son the way Teena had? he asked himself for the thousandth time. But he had no answer. Women were a mystery to him. He'd long given up trying to understand them. All he wanted was to keep his son safe and happy. So even if he'd rather stay away from Monique, Calvin's happiness took priority. And, right now, it seemed Monique made him happy. "Look, Ma, like I told you already, Calvin and I ran into Monique over at the school. Calvin liked her, so I invited her to have ice cream with us."

"You invited her?" his mother interrupted. She pulled off her glasses and let them hang from the gold chain around her neck. Dillon knew this meant the subject had her full attention. "You never told us that. You made it sound like she just tagged along. Why did you invite her?"

Dillon looked at his watch. Why was it taking his father and Calvin so long to walk around the block?

"He invited her because he wanted her company, Ma," Donald answered for his brother. "I, for one, am glad he did. I always liked Monique."

"You were the only one," his mother said. She lifted her right hand and wagged her index finger in the air. "I knew that girl was trouble the first day I met her. And she broke your brother's heart just like I thought she would."

Dillon stood up, tired of listening to his mother and brother talk about him as if he weren't in the room. "I'm going to meet Dad and Calvin. I need to get Calvin home and to bed."

His mother stood and followed him to the door. "There's no need for you to leave now. You never leave this soon after we eat."

"Well, I have to get up early in the morning,"

Dillon said, not slowing down. He knew that if he stayed, he'd be subject to more discussion about him and Monique. Not exactly the way he wanted to spend the evening.

"Are you sure?" his mother asked.

"I'm sure, Ma." He turned and kissed her on the cheek. "Good night, Ma. I love you."

"I know you do, son," his mother said in response. "You're a good boy, Dillon. Now be careful driving home. And tell your father to give Calvin a big hug for me."

"Okay," he said, stepping out of the screen door and onto the porch. "I'll tell him."

Dillon hopped off the porch into the now cool August evening. When he reached the sidewalk, he took the reverse of the route that his father and Calvin had taken, hoping he'd run into them on their way back to the house.

As he walked down the street that had been his childhood playground, thoughts of Monique rushed to the surface. Thoughts that had been long suppressed. God, how he'd loved that girl.

She'd been everything he thought he could ever want in a woman, a wife. And, in his youthful innocence, he'd thought they would spend the rest of their lives together. How quickly that dream had turned into a nightmare.

Monique had been talking about the senior prom all year. She'd said that she wanted it to be a night they'd always remember. He sighed the sigh of the weary. Well, she'd gotten her wish. That night was etched in his brain and he'd never forget it.

He could still feel the panic he'd felt when he'd

gone to her house to pick her up and her aunt had answered the door.

"She's gone," her aunt had said. "Took her suitcases and just left."

At first he'd thought he'd heard wrong, but the woman repeated her words.

"But she can't be gone," he'd tried to explain. "Tonight is Prom Night."

"She didn't care about any prom," the aunt had said with a shake of her head. "That dress of hers is still in her room."

Those words had sent Dillon rushing past the older woman and up the stairs to Monique's bedroom. Just as the aunt had said, Monique's blue-and-white gown was on the bed. He hadn't known what to think, so he'd rushed back downstairs and questioned her aunt some more.

"Where'd she go?" he'd asked, all the while feeling panic rise in his throat. She couldn't have gone and left him. She would never do that to him, he'd naively thought.

Monique's aunt had just shrugged her shoulders, making him want to shake her. "She couldn't have just left," he said aloud. "What did she say?"

"Didn't say nothing," the old woman had said. "But she did leave you a note on the table over there."

Dillon had rushed to the end table next to the couch. When he'd seen the flat envelope with his name on it, he ripped open the pale beige envelope and snatched out the letter.

As he read the terse words from the girl he'd loved more than his own life, the bottom dropped out of his world.

Chapter Two

"I gotta go, Mom." The words rushed out of young Glenn's mouth. "Jonathan's dad's taking us to see Michael Jordan. We're gonna get autographs and everything."

"All right, then, go on," Monique said, hoping her disappointment didn't reflect in her voice and carry through the phone line. Her nine-year-old was growing up. She didn't know if she liked that. "But Glenn—"

"Aw, Mom…"

"Don't 'Aw, Mom,' me. You listen to Jonathan's dad and don't give him any trouble. Do you hear me?"

She imagined him tapping the heel of his sneaker against the floor, his trademark motion of impatience. "I hear you, Mom. Can I go now?"

"May I go," she automatically corrected.

"Okay, may I go now?"

She sighed. "Yes, you may. I love you, Glenn, and I'll see you soon."

"I love you, too, Mom." Glenn parroted her words without much thought. "Here's Aunt Sue. I gotta go."

Monique heard Sue's last-minute instructions for Glenn's behavior. She knew she had nothing to worry about when Glenn was with her sister-in-law, but that didn't keep Monique from worrying. Recently, Glenn had been having problems that she knew were related to his missing his father. It had been three years since Charles's death, but the doctors had said Glenn's delayed reaction was normal. They'd said he was at the age when he needed a father most, and it was only natural that he act out.

"Whew," came Sue's tired voice. "Sorry about that, Monique."

"Did he have a bad day today?" she asked, wishing she weren't three hundred miles away from her baby. "He's not giving you any trouble, is he?"

"Not really, but then you know Glenn can be a handful even on his good days."

The affection in Sue's voice helped Monique to relax because she knew it meant Glenn was having a good day. "Right now, Sue, he could be Attila the Hun and I wouldn't complain. I miss my baby."

Sue laughed and the clear, happy sound made Monique smile. Sue's happiness had that effect on people. "You'd better not let Glenn hear you call him a baby. Somebody must have told him he was a little man because that's exactly the way he's acting."

Sue's words made Monique miss her son even

more. "I need him with me, Sue. We've never been apart before."

Sue seemed to sober quickly. "I know that, but I also know that you have to do some heavy-duty preparation work before you can bring Glenn to Elberton. Have you made any progress?"

Monique's fingers traced the buttons on the telephone keypad. "I saw Dillon today."

"Well, that was quick. What happened?"

"Nothing much. We went for ice cream. I met his son."

"His *other* son, you mean," Sue corrected.

"Whatever," Monique retorted. "His name's Calvin and he's a wonderful four-year-old, a lot like Glenn was at his age. He even let me hold his hand. I can't remember the last time Glenn voluntarily let me hold his hand."

Sue's silence spoke volumes. Monique knew her sister-in-law was waiting for her to talk about Dillon, not his son. Unfortunately, Monique found talking about Calvin pleasurable, while talking about Dillon made her sad.

"Dillon's still angry," Monique said after a few more moments of silence. "I don't blame him, but it hurts to know that I'm responsible for his anger. He couldn't get away from me fast enough at the ice-cream shop. I don't know how he's going to take my news."

"He'll be surprised. Probably angry at first, but he'll come around."

Leave it to Sue to respond to a rhetorical statement with reason. It was another trait that Monique admired in her. "I wish I could be as confident as you are."

"You'll be fine, Monique. Don't worry so."

Monique smiled. "What did I do to deserve a wonderful sister like you?"

"You married my brother and you took care of him," Sue responded. "I'll always owe you for that. You and Glenn made the last few years of Charles's life worth living."

Tears formed in Monique's eyes. "Charles was good to me, too, Sue. It wasn't all one-sided."

"I know the sacrifice you made for my brother, Monique, and I don't know if I could have made that same sacrifice had I been in your position. You're a good woman, a good person, and because of all the good you've done, you're due to reap more goodness. Trust me."

Monique wished she could, but she didn't have Sue's optimism. She'd grown up knowing that if she stood a fifty-fifty chance of having *good* luck, she'd definitely have *bad* luck. She could have been the poster child for Murphy's Law. If something bad *could* happen, it definitely *would* happen to her.

Though she'd married Charles to save Dillon from the disaster she was so sure she would ultimately bring to his life, she'd come to care deeply for the older man. He'd encouraged her to become a person she could be proud of.

She'd gotten her advanced degree in education and found a career that she thought was perfect for her. And, most importantly, she'd learned to be a good mother to her son. She'd been afraid a lot at first, but over time she'd come to accept that she could love and care for a baby. And that she could do it well. She had Charles to thank for that, too.

But when Charles had gotten ill, some of her newly found optimism about life and what it had to offer her had wavered. Though she knew she hadn't been the cause of Charles's illness or his death, she felt that the Fates had played a horrible trick on her. They'd allowed her to hope and then they'd tried to take her to the depths of despair, but her love for Glenn and the knowledge that he needed her had kept her sane and steady. It was because of Glenn that she was back in Elberton.

"I don't know what I'd do without you, Sue," Monique said after a long pause. "You're the sister I never had."

"The same goes for me, Monique. We're family and we'll always be. Don't you ever forget that."

"I won't," Monique said, close to tears again. "Look, I'd better get off this phone. I'm going to need all of my energy for my talk with Dillon."

"Well, I'll let you go so you can get some sleep. And don't worry so much. Things will work out for you and Dillon. Just keep believing that."

"I'm not looking for things to work out between me and Dillon," Monique corrected. "I've told you that. I just want him and Glenn to have a relationship. I owe my son that much."

"If you say so, but I know you better than that. I've watched you turn away man after man for some flimsy reason or another—"

"That's not true," Monique interrupted. "I just haven't met the right man."

"And you won't until you get over Dillon. You still love him, Monique."

Monique sighed. There was no use arguing with Sue. They'd had this conversation many times before, and she knew she couldn't win. "I guess we're at a stalemate on this topic. Again."

Sue chuckled. "That's all right. You'll come around."

"Sue!"

"Good night, Monique. Keep me posted."

Monique said good-night with a grim smile on her face. She couldn't afford to be swayed by Sue's optimism. The fact was that she and Dillon had a past, but only Dillon and Glenn had a future. She'd have to remember that, because she knew if she forgot it, the Fates would find some cruel way of reminding her.

Monique dropped down on a weather-beaten bench at the park around the block from the last rental she'd visited. Though it was only noon, she'd already viewed six houses and one apartment. Nothing she'd seen compared to the house she was leaving behind, but the house she'd just seen, a sprawling colonial, did have potential for a short-term stay. It was within walking distance of the park and the elementary school where Glenn would be enrolled. It could work.

She rubbed her hands down her denim-encased legs and hunched her shoulders together, working the kinks out of her back. She'd been in Elberton two days and already she was stressed out. At the rate she was going, she'd be a basket case before she got around to giving Dillon her news.

"Moni! Moni!"

Monique looked up in the direction of the familiar voice. She smiled and opened her arms when she saw Calvin and Dillon coming her way. Again the twosome were dressed in matching shorts. Calvin's short legs pumped furiously as he rushed toward her, obviously glad to see her. When he was about three feet from her, he launched himself into her arms.

"Hold on there, slugger," Dillon called, leaning forward to pull Calvin off Monique. "You're going to hurt somebody."

"It's Moni," Calvin said with a grin. "Hi, Moni. We're going to the lake. Wanna come? We're gonna catch some fish."

Monique turned up her nose. "I don't think I want to go fishing."

Calvin's lips turned down in disappointment. "'Cuz you're a girl?"

Monique fought back a smile. She knew an affirmative answer to that question would definitely lower her stock in the young boy's eyes. She tweaked his nose. "No. Because I don't have a fishing pole."

"Oh," Calvin said, his brows bunched together as if he were thinking of a solution to her problem. When his eyes widened and his broad grin returned, Monique knew he'd found one. "You can use my pole. I can show you."

Monique smiled at the little boy. A part of her wanted to go fishing with Dillon and him, but another part of her didn't feel comfortable spending time with them when she held a secret that would drastically affect their lives. She looked down at Calvin's smiling face then back up at Dillon's.

Dillon saw the question in her eyes and the hope in Calvin's. "Come with us," he said. "Calvin's a good fisherman. He'll teach you well."

"You're sure?" she asked, undecided on which action to take.

He nodded. "I'm sure. You've woven your spell

around another Bell man, and there's nothing I can do about it."

His anger was still there, she knew. Though she didn't hear it in the tone of his voice, it was there in those dark, hooded eyes of his. What was he thinking? she wondered. Did he hate her? Would he hate her more when he found out her secret?

"So what's it going to be?" Dillon asked.

She smiled down at Calvin and the hope in the little boy's eyes decided for her. "Are you ready to give me my first fishing lesson?"

After about two hours on the lake with Calvin, Dillon and the mosquitoes, Monique was ready to admit she'd made the wrong decision. Fishing was definitely not the sport for her. She preferred professional basketball. Held *indoors* in an air-conditioned building. She looked back over her shoulder at her fishing teacher, now asleep in the shade directly behind the bank where she and Dillon sat. She wanted more than anything to join him, as much to get away from the strained silence between her and Dillon as to get away from the mosquitoes. She turned away from the sleeping Calvin and focused her attention on trying to kill at least one of the thousands of mosquitoes that had decided she made for good eating.

"You should use some more of the spray." Dillon's flat voice broke the silence between them. "Those mosquitoes seem to like you."

She batted at another one of the beasts and missed. "I know now why I never fished before. When did you start?" What she wanted to ask was why the bothersome insects spared him their attention. The man looked too comfortable for words sitting there in his plaid knee-length shorts and red T-shirt as if he didn't have a care in the world. If they had a relationship that was anywhere in shaking distance of a friendship, she'd push him in the lake.

"The summer after high school graduation," he said in answer to her question. "I spent a lot of time out here thinking. Fishing is a solitary sport even when you're with people. I needed time alone."

Monique took a deep breath. This was the opening she'd been waiting for. "I'm sorry, Dillon. I'm so sorry."

He shrugged his wide shoulders, causing the material of his shirt to stretch taut across his broad chest. "Like I told you before, that's the past. We have to live in the present."

"You make it sound so simple."

"It is. Thinking about it, regretting your actions, won't change anything. We were young and thought we were in love. We were wrong. We weren't the first teenage lovers to learn that, and we certainly weren't the last."

She sucked in her breath at the dispassion in his words. Was he saying he'd never really loved her? "I think it's more complicated than that."

"Only because you want it to be. What do you want anyway, Monique? Why did you come back here? I know that when you left you had no plans to return. Why this sudden case of conscience?"

Was she that obvious? "What makes you think I've had a 'sudden case of conscience,' as you put it?"

He propped his fishing pole on the bank and leaned back on his elbows. "The last time I saw you—before yesterday—was ten years ago, and I haven't heard anything from you in all that time. Not a single word.

It was as if you forgot everybody and everything. You just disappeared."

Dillon's words were controlled, softly spoken. If she hadn't known him as well as she did, she would have thought he was unaffected by his accusation. But she *knew* him—even after all the time that had passed—and she knew his anger was rising with his every word. How could she make him understand the choice she'd made back then? One unwise decision had mushroomed into a lie that now affected many innocent lives. "It was more complicated than that, Dillon" was all she could say.

"I bet it was," he said, his words laced with sarcasm. "I bet it was real complicated when you packed up and slipped out of town leaving only that 'I'm gone' letter behind." He focused his eyes on his fishing pole. "I was a fool. I actually thought you loved me, and all the while you were just passing time until you could make your grand getaway from Elberton. I never meant anything to you."

It's not true, she wanted to say. *I loved you with all my heart.* But she couldn't start a conversation now that they couldn't finish. "We need to talk, Dillon." She glanced back at the sleeping Calvin. "In private."

"You aren't listening to me, are you, Monique? The past is best left in the past. Talking about it will only bring back memories better left buried."

She shook her head. "I can't let this go. We have to talk. *I* have to talk. There are some things you should know."

"I don't—"

She placed a hand on his knee. "Please, Dillon, do

this for me. Just hear me out. This is something I need to do."

He pushed her hand away, knowing he wasn't immune to her touch, then leaned toward her until his nose was within inches of hers. "And why should I give a damn about what you need? The only reason you're here now is because Calvin has found something in you he likes. If it were left up to me, we'd only see each other when necessary. And I've lived without you long enough to know it would never be necessary for me to see you."

Monique opened her mouth to speak, but Calvin stirred from his sleep. She lowered her voice. "We're going to talk, Dillon. Sooner or later, we're going to talk."

"Hot date?" Donald asked after using his key to unlock Dillon's front door. Dillon noticed a smudge of red against the side of his brother's mouth. Lipstick, what else? His brother still had on his police uniform, but the lipstick said he'd made a stop since ending his shift. "Must have come up suddenly if you need me to baby-sit."

Dillon didn't bother to comment on the lipstick or to answer his brother's question. He went back to his bedroom to get his shirt. Too bad Donald followed him.

"Calvin asleep?" Donald asked, now leaning against the cedar chest near Dillon's bedroom door.

"Out like a light. He won't wake up until morning. Fishing tired him out."

His brother grinned and Dillon turned away. That grin could only mean bad things for him.

"So I heard," Donald said. "Another threesome, was it?"

Small-town living, Dillon thought. Some people needed to get a life. "She went with us."

"You invited her *again?*"

Dillon looked up at his brother. The grin was still there right along with that stupid smudge of lipstick. "Look, I asked you to sit with Calvin, not come here and give me the third degree." He quickly fastened the buttons on his shirt and tucked it into his jeans. No need to dress up. This wasn't a date.

"Nice-smelling cologne you have on," Donald commented. Dillon didn't have to look at his brother to know that he was still wearing that foolish grin. "Must be serious."

Dillon frowned at his brother. "What's that supposed to mean?"

Donald lifted both hands as if to ward off any blows. "Nothing, bro. No need to get all huffy on me. I didn't mean anything by the comment." He dropped his gaze as if hurt by Dillon's question. "I was just thinking that this must be some special lady for you to go see her on such short notice. You don't usually leave the house after Calvin's asleep."

Dillon grimaced as he watched his brother fake being hurt. Donald had been playing these games since they were children. He wondered when his younger brother would grow up and stop kidding around. "Forget it, Donald. I'm not falling for that 'you hurt my feelings' routine." He strode out of the bedroom past his brother. "You know the drill," he said as he opened the front door. "And don't set up house in my bedroom. I'll be back soon." He stepped through the door and out of the house.

"Not if you're lucky," Donald muttered.

Dillon stopped and looked back at his brother. "What did you say?" he asked, though he'd heard clearly.

Donald coughed what had to be the worst pretend cough Dillon had ever heard. "I said be careful."

Dillon stared at his brother for a long second before shaking his head. "I won't be long. Don't wreck my house before I get back. And wipe that stupid lipstick off your face."

Dillon closed the door and quickly crossed his wide porch to the steps. He bought this house after he'd been awarded full custody of Calvin, thinking the boy needed a house with a porch and his own yard instead of a couple of rooms in an apartment building. His mother had wanted him and Calvin to move back home, but Dillon didn't like the idea of a twenty-eight-year-old man with a son moving back in with his parents. So, he'd found the house instead. With his mother's help—and that of a few of the single young ladies in Elberton—his three-bedroom single-level house was now home for him and Calvin. His mother came over twice a week to make sure they had food and clean clothes. Other than that, he and Calvin roughed it.

Dillon climbed into the cab of the red pickup he'd bought a couple of months ago. Though he much preferred basic black, he'd given in to his son's preference and gotten the red. There wasn't much he wouldn't do to see a genuine smile on Calvin's face. As he'd told Monique earlier, the smile she put on the boy's face was the only reason she was *in* his life now instead of on the periphery of it.

He was still trying to figure out what about her

caused Calvin to respond the way he did. If the boy were a teenager, he would guess he was responding to Monique as a member of the opposite sex, but four-year-old Calvin wouldn't know opposite sex from a hole in the wall. So what was it about Monique that made his son happy?

Dillon didn't want to think about the ways she'd made him happy in the past, but the thoughts came anyway. As he let those memories surround him, he realized that back then he'd been a lot like Calvin was now. Monique didn't have to *do* anything to make him happy; just her presence did it for him. He couldn't explain it then and he couldn't explain it now. His feelings for Monique didn't come from reason. Reason would have told him that he and Monique were too different in temperament to have a lasting relationship. Monique had been hotheaded then, almost to the point of being cruel. But there was something about her, something fragile and pure that was in contradiction with her volatility, something that touched him as he'd never been touched before. Or since.

She was different now, though. He could tell her brashness was gone, but he didn't know what had replaced it. He didn't intend to find out, either. No, he'd been Monique's victim once. As his mother always said, ''Fool me once, shame on you. Fool me twice, shame on me.'' No, he wasn't about to be the fool twice.

He ignored the quiet voice from inside himself that asked, ''Then why are you driving over to see her?''

Chapter Three

"Good night, sweetheart. I love you." Monique whispered the words over the phone to her son whom she missed desperately.

"Night, Mom." Glenn yawned, then added, "Love you, too."

Sadness settled around Monique as she hung up the phone. Her baby was growing up. It's not fair, she thought, he's only nine years old. He needed to remain her baby for a while longer. For her sake.

She glanced at the clock on her nightstand. Only nine o'clock and she was already in bed. Too bad she wasn't sleepy. Though sleep would be preferable to its alternative: hours and hours of thinking about Dillon and what could have been.

She wondered what he was doing now. She supposed he'd put Calvin to bed and was getting ready for bed himself, but she couldn't be sure. Maybe he had a date. She'd assumed he wasn't seriously involved with anyone since both times she'd seen him and Calvin they'd been alone. And as much as Calvin talked, had there been a woman in their lives, she was sure the boy would have mentioned her by now.

No, Calvin made Monique feel as though she were *the* woman in their lives. And she liked the feeling even though she knew it was only a dream. A dream she'd been having in one form or another since her teenage days when she and Dillon had planned for marriage and a family with four children—two boys and two girls. She'd even started picking out names for them, but Dillon had convinced her to save some of the fun until after they were married and she was pregnant.

The bittersweet memory of that long-ago time soothed her. Those nights of loving talks had been some of the most important nights of her life. They'd helped her get through hardships no teenager should have had to face. And after she'd made the decision that had forever relegated her dreams to the realm of fantasy, those memories had sustained her.

If she could do it all over again, she thought, she'd—

A rap at her front door brought her out of her imaginings. Who could that be? she wondered. It wasn't as if she'd been in contact with anyone other than Dillon and Calvin, and she hadn't even told them that she was staying in one of the one-bedroom rental units above the furniture store.

But this was Elberton and there weren't that many choices for temporary living. She got up from the bed, slipped on her robe and slid her feet into her house shoes, then rushed to the door. By the time she reached it, the knocks had turned to pounding. "Just a minute," she yelled in impatience. "You don't have to break down the door."

She raised herself up on her toes and peeked out the peephole. The sight made her breath catch in her throat. It was Dillon. And he looked anxious. And gorgeous. And all he was doing was leaning against her wall. She lowered herself, pulled her robe tighter around her, brushed her hand across her head, then took a deep breath. You can handle this, she told herself as she pulled the door open.

"Dillon," she said, and felt like a fool. He knew who he was.

He moved away from the door frame and stood to his full six-foot height. "You said you wanted to talk. I'm here. Talk."

So much for pleasantries, she thought. She stepped back. "We'd better do this inside."

He strode past her and she closed her eyes and savored the masculine scent of his cologne. He even smelled strong. Her eyes shot open. What the heck was she doing?

She followed Dillon into the living area and invited him to sit on the sofa. She sat in the chair next to it.

"So talk," he said again.

She had no doubt he just wanted to get the task done so he could go home and get on with his life. It wasn't going to be that easy, though. For either of them. "Would you like something to drink? I have soda or I could put on a pot of coffee?"

Dillon shook his head, his eyes pinned to hers. He refused to let his gaze drop from her face, though he wanted more than anything to know if she were naked beneath her robe. He'd seen the slope of her breasts when she opened the door, so he knew she wasn't wearing a bra. And when she'd sat down, her robe had gaped open, giving him a view of her nice firm thighs. If she had on a nightgown, it was a skimpy one. "I didn't come here for refreshments. You said we needed to talk. So talk."

She tried to ignore the pain his disinterest caused her. "What made you come?" she asked.

He allowed his eyes to drop to her chest for a quick moment. "I felt I owed you. Calvin likes you a lot and you've been nice to him. I felt I owed you for being nice to my boy."

So he was here out of his sense of gratitude. So like the honorable Dillon she'd always known. He should change his name to "Do the Right Thing" Dillon.

"You don't owe me for being nice to Calvin. He's a sweet little boy and I like him a lot. I enjoy being around him."

He folded his arms across his chest and flattened his lips in a tight line. Why did she have to be so beautiful? Why did he have to notice? "What did you want to talk about? I don't have all night."

The coldness of his words wrapped around her heart and she shivered. "Do you hate me so much that you can't bear to be alone with me?"

He dropped his eyes from hers and breathed a deep breath. "I don't hate you, Monique. I stopped hating you years ago."

"You act as though you still hate me," she said, not believing his words. "Your body language says you're angry and closed."

"I'm not angry," he repeated, dropping his folded arms. "I'm just curious about your reasons for coming back to Elberton." And concerned that you still have the power to affect my senses, he added to himself.

"You don't buy that I came back for the job at the school?"

His lips now turned in a solid smirk. "I've seen your résumé. You could have written a ticket for any job you wanted in any place that you wanted. What I don't know is why you picked Elberton."

"It's my home," she said, stalling for time.

"Yeah, right. Look, Monique, like I said, I don't have all night. If you've got something you want to say, say it. I didn't come here for small talk."

Well, she guessed he'd told her. She cleared her throat. "I'm sorry, Dillon. I'm so sorry."

He rubbed his large hands down his thighs and sighed again. "You've said that three times now. You have nothing to be sorry for. We were kids. Kids can't be held responsible for their actions. You're a parent. You should know that."

She shook her head. "No, I don't know that. What we had was more than kid stuff, Dillon. At least, it was for me."

He blinked. She waited for him to say something but the single blink was his only response.

"I loved you, Dillon. With all of my heart, I loved you."

His ears burned with her words. "How can you say that to me, Monique?" he asked, his voice dangerously low and controlled. "How can you say you loved me after the way you ended our relationship?"

"You don't understand, Dillon—"

"Damn right, I don't understand. I don't understand how a woman can love a man one day, skip out of town on him the next and then be married and pregnant with another's man baby a few months later. Damn straight, I don't understand."

Though Monique had known her actions would hurt Dillon, she hadn't realized until now how cold-blooded they had seemed to him. Hearing him describe what had happened made her actions seem indefensible, even to her. "I know I hurt you—"

"Hurt me?" He shook his head, his lips twisted in a snarl. "Do you know how many nights I lay awake wondering if you'd been sneaking around behind my back while I was playing knight in shining armor and protecting your virtue?"

"I wasn't sneaking around behind your back, Dillon," Monique said softly. "I never slept with anyone but you."

He laughed, a harsh sound that rang in her ears like the howl of a wounded animal. "Look, I may not have learned much about women over the years, but my understanding of basic biology is clear. You were pregnant with his baby, Monique. How did you manage that without sleeping with him?"

His pain became her pain. He was angry, but more important to her was the pain and the hurt that she heard in his voice. He'd loved her and she'd tossed his love back in his face. "It wasn't his baby." There. She'd said it.

Dillon's eyes widened. "It wasn't his baby?" he repeated.

She shook her head slowly, waiting for understanding to appear in his eyes.

"You're lying," he said. "You're lying."

She knew he understood. She could see it in his eyes, along with the disbelief. "I lied then, Dillon, but I'm not lying now. Though Charles raised Glenn as his own, you're his biological father."

His heart slammed around in his chest, and his breathing became difficult. "What did you say?" he asked. She couldn't have said what he thought she'd said. Maybe he'd misunderstood her or missed something in the conversation. He'd been having a difficult time concentrating on her words with her dressed in that robe.

"I was pregnant with *your* son, not Charles's."

He shook his head to clear his mind and his ears. "My son?"

She nodded and nervously ran her hand through her hair. He wondered if it was as soft as he remembered. Stupid thought, given what she'd just told him, but a much easier thought to entertain than the news that she'd given his son to another man. He looked at this woman he'd loved with all his heart and wondered if he'd ever really known her. "Why should I believe you?"

"Why should I lie?"

"Why *did* you lie?" he returned.

She got up from her chair, pulling her robe tight around her from her neck to where it fell midthigh. "Wait right here," she said, then left the room.

He snorted. Where the hell did she think he was going? She was back before he could answer his own question.

"Here," she said, handing him two gold-framed eight-by-ten photographs.

Before he looked at them, he knew they were of her son, Glenn. After he looked at them, he knew without doubt that Glenn was his son, too. The boy in one of the photos could have been Calvin, except for his skin color. Calvin was a shade or two lighter than the dark-brown-skinned Glenn. The second frame held a photo, probably taken recently, of an older Glenn. Dillon knew he'd looked much like the boy at that same age.

He studied the photos longer than necessary to keep from looking at Monique. He didn't know what he'd do if he looked at her. What kind of woman deceived not one man, but two? And what about Glenn? What was this going to do to his son?

"I found out I was pregnant a week or so before the senior prom. I was happy and scared at the same time." Those two emotions had dogged her for years. First, because of the pregnancy. Later, because of her lie. "You know how much I wanted your baby."

Her voice grated on him, but he didn't look at her. He couldn't. Not yet. He'd thought he couldn't hurt worse than the day he'd learned she was married and pregnant, but now he knew he was wrong.

"I know this is a shock, Dillon, and I can imagine what you must think about me—"

He looked up at her then. Her flinch told him that she correctly read the disgust in his eyes.

"My actions weren't as coldhearted as they seem," she continued. "I didn't tell you about the baby because I didn't want you to be saddled with a family before you were ready."

He laughed, a hollow sound this time. "Let me get this straight, Monique. You lied to me and gave my son to another man because you were thinking of me. Do I have it right?"

"You have it right, but you still don't understand."

Dillon understood, all right. He understood everything. His understanding had become clear that afternoon ten years ago when he'd found her, pregnant and married, in Charleston, three hundred miles from Elberton. When she'd told him she was married, he'd gone into shock. At first he hadn't believed her, then she'd uttered the words that had killed whatever love he'd had for her. "I'm pregnant with his baby," she'd said, referring to the man with her. He'd had no response for that bombshell. He'd staggered away from her and the man who'd been old enough to be her father and gone home to heal. It had taken him years, and though he'd known he would never get over her and what she'd done to him, he'd put it in perspective and moved on.

And now she was bringing it all back. All the hurt and all the distrust. He had a son. A son he'd been denied for nine years.

He glanced up at her and saw the tears in her eyes. Why was she was crying when he was the injured party? he wondered, fighting the irrational urge to comfort her.

She wiped at her tears, then stood up, unnecessarily tugging at her robe. "I only told you it was his baby to make you leave. I didn't want me and my baby to be a burden to you."

Dillon thought he was in some place resembling the twilight zone. "What are you talking about?"

Her tears flowed freely now and he steeled his heart against them. "I was so scared, Dillon. All my life my aunt had told me what a burden I was. I can still hear her telling me that. She blamed my mother for dumping me off on her, and she accused me of ruining my mother's life. I was tired of being a burden, and I couldn't let my baby become anybody's burden. I couldn't do that to my child, Dillon. I just couldn't."

"You thought I wouldn't want you and the baby? How could you think that, Monique? I loved you and I would have loved our baby."

She smiled a sad smile. "I know you loved me, Dillon, and that's why I had to do what I did."

"This is not making sense. You left me because I loved you?"

"Don't you see?" she pleaded. "I knew you wouldn't leave me. I trusted your love that much. So I had to leave you. That's why I married Charles and that's why I told you I was pregnant with his baby. I had to do something, say something, that would get you out of my life so that you could have a life. You loved me then, but soon you would have blamed me for the changes a wife and baby made in your life. I couldn't have handled watching your love for me die, Dillon. You were all I had and I loved you too much."

"So you're saying that you lied to me because you loved me?" His words dripped with sarcasm. "Either you're crazy or I'm crazy because that makes absolutely no sense to me."

"It made sense to me," she said. "Let's be realistic, Dillon. What would you, a high school student, have done with a wife and child?"

"Because of you, we'll never know." He stared at her, wondering what had been going through her mind when she'd made her decision. He knew the sadness he saw on her face mirrored the sadness on his own. He shook his head, then quickly scrambled to his feet. He couldn't be with her anymore. He was going to start yelling or he was going to pull her into his arms and comfort her. Neither act was appropriate.

"I've got to get out of here. I can't talk about this anymore."

He placed the framed photos on the table, then walked to the door. He reached for the knob, then released it and went back to the table. He picked up the frames and his gaze met hers. "He's my son," he said. Then he took the photos and left her apartment.

Monique stood staring at the door for a long while after Dillon had gone. She'd told him the truth, and, as expected, she'd hurt him all over again. It didn't help her to know that it would have been more cruel to keep her secret. She only hoped that one day he'd understand her motivations and forgive her lies.

She rubbed her hands up and down her arms, chilly though the room was warm. She'd told him. Now the next move was his. She would just have to wait until he made it.

Dillon parked his truck a block away from his house. He had to compose himself before going home or Donald would know something was wrong and badger him until he found out what it was. He knew he had to share his news with his family, but he wasn't ready to do that yet. He had to find some place of understanding, some position from which he could stand, or this would break him.

There was no use lying to himself any longer. Monique was the only person in the world who could hurt him this way. She'd had that power ten years ago, and she still had it today. A part of him wished he'd never known her. Yet, even after all the hurt she'd caused him, another part of him knew that loving her was an experience he wouldn't have wanted to miss.

He just hated that his love had been wasted on a woman who had twice proven herself unworthy.

He turned the knob for the truck's interior light and picked up the most recent photo of Glenn. His son. His oldest boy. Tears formed in his own eyes now as he thought about the child he'd never known. How would the boy handle all this? And Calvin. How would this affect him?

Dillon didn't want to think how different his life would have been if Monique had told him the truth. He knew they would have married immediately. The baby, though unplanned, would have been welcomed with love. He and Monique had often talked about children. She'd known how badly he wanted to see her grow large with his baby. He'd told her often enough.

But though he'd believed in Monique and their love, she hadn't believed in him. Not enough to trust him and his love when it mattered most. Not enough to tell him about their child and give him a chance to participate in whatever decisions had needed to be made. She'd had so little trust in him that she'd given his child to another man. He couldn't think of a greater betrayal.

"You definitely have a way with women," he told himself. "One woman takes your son and leaves you, while another one deserts both you and your son."

Dillon shook his head. He didn't understand women and he knew now that he never would. All he knew was that he'd been dealt a tough hand, but a hand he was determined to play. He had to, because he loved his sons. Both of them.

Chapter Four

Monique was already awake when her alarm clock went off at seven o'clock the next morning. She turned and pressed the snooze button, then lay on her back, her arms folded across her stomach. Right now, she felt very much alone. As alone as she'd felt ten years ago when she'd made the difficult and heart-breaking decision to leave Elberton without telling Dillon about her pregnancy.

Though her decision had been a tough one, she had been convinced at the time it was the right one. For her, for Dillon and for their baby. She could still hear her aunt's hate-filled words. "I hope you don't end up like your momma," she'd said. "She was too young to know what to do with a baby and that boy she was running around with wasn't any better."

By the time Monique was twelve years old, she'd known the shame and heartache her birth had caused her mother. "Having a baby ruined both their lives," her aunt often told her. "And after your father ran out on her, your momma just couldn't take it. So one day she comes to visit me then sneaks out in the middle of the night, leaving you here." Monique heard the words now as if her aunt were again speaking to her. "What did I want with a baby?"

Tears again filled Monique's eyes. She couldn't have put Dillon in the situation of having a baby he didn't really want. Sure, they'd talked about having a baby, but they'd always talked about sometime in the future. After they'd finished college and after they'd gotten married. They hadn't said anything about a baby in high school. Young and in love, they hadn't even considered the possibility.

But she'd had to face the reality when she'd learned she was pregnant. And she had known that life with a baby would be drastically different from life without one. For her, it had meant college was out of the question. She hadn't seen any way she could go to college *and* take care of her baby. The thought of her aunt helping out never crossed her mind. If anything, she hadn't wanted her aunt's viciousness to touch her baby's life. No, she'd wanted to protect her unborn child and Dillon.

Oh, God, Dillon, I loved you so much, she thought as tears rolled down her cheeks. I loved you so much.

She wiped at her tears and tried to get a grip on her emotions. You've got to stop looking back, she told herself. Think about your son. He's the reason you're back here.

Dear, sweet, miserable Glenn. She knew her son was hurting. And he had been hurting ever since Charles had died. The two had been so close that it pained her to think how much Glenn missed Charles. They'd been father and son. Buddies. Friends. She could only imagine the empty space that now existed in her son's heart. She knew even before his doctor had told her that Glenn's erratic behavior, his surliness and the drastic change in his personality were just ways of filling the void left by Charles's death.

Things had seemed to get better when she signed him up for the Big Brother program, but that had soon worn off. The day after the first time his Big Brother had called to cancel a planned outing, Glenn had gotten into a fight at school. She'd been horrified when the principal had called her with the news. Then she'd known it was time to tell Dillon the truth. Glenn needed a man he could count on in his life. He needed a father. His father.

Monique groaned then sat up in bed. She wished she could stay here all day. But she knew she had to face the day and Dillon. And his anger. Not that she blamed him for being angry. She didn't. She just hadn't realized how much his anger would hurt her. And she hadn't realized just how much she still loved him.

Tossing those thoughts aside, she climbed out of bed. A knock at her front door sounded just as she was about to step into the shower. She grabbed her robe, sucked in her breath and braced herself for another round with Dillon. She pulled open the door without checking the peephole and was surprised to find not Dillon, but his younger brother, Donald.

"Guess you were expecting someone else," he said, wearing the same charming Bell smile that his older brother wore. Donald had broken a lot of hearts in his day and she imagined he still did. He looked quite the hunk in his navy police uniform.

"Hi, Donald," she said, wondering what he was doing at her place. Had Dillon already told him about Glenn? Though Donald had been the one member of the Bell family, other than Dillon, who genuinely liked her, she wondered if her secret would change his opinion. "This is a real surprise. When did you become a police officer?"

He leaned against her doorjamb. "Somebody has to make the world safe for women and children. I thought I'd give it a shot."

She stepped back from the door. "Do you want to come in for a few minutes? I have an appointment at the school this morning, but I have some time now."

"No, I don't want to intrude," Donald said. "Besides, I'm on my way to work. Early shift today. I just wanted to stop by and welcome you back to Elberton."

"Why, thank you, Donald." She realized then that his were her first real words of welcome. Dillon's halfhearted words that day at the ice-cream shop had been spoken in sarcasm. "It was so nice of you to come all the way over here just to tell me that," she said, pushing away her troubled thoughts.

He gave a sheepish smile that reminded her of his brother. "Well, I'd heard you were back in town and I wanted to see you for myself."

She wondered what else he'd heard. "I'm definitely back."

"And looking just as pretty as ever."

"You're flirting with me," she said with a smile. "I don't believe you, Donald Bell."

Donald grinned. "I've always flirted with you,

Monique. I flirted with every girl Dillon and Darnell dated. Of course, none of you took me seriously."

Monique enjoyed the memories with a smile. "And you would have been hurt if we had. We all knew the Bell brothers were a team."

"And that's why I liked flirting with you." Donald stood to his full height, which was only a couple of inches shorter than his brother. "I guess I'd better go. I don't want to be late for work."

"Thanks again, Donald," she said. "I appreciate your stopping by. Don't be a stranger."

He grinned down at her as if he knew something that she didn't. "Somehow I don't think that's going to be a problem. See you around, Monique."

As Monique closed the door, she wondered what Donald's grin and cryptic words meant. Did he think she and Dillon were seeing each other again? She certainly hoped not. All she needed now was for the Bells to think she was making a play for their son. They'd be in enough shock once they found out about Glenn.

She shook her head to clear her thoughts. Then she went to get dressed for her meeting at the school.

Dillon went through the motions of getting Calvin ready for day care. When the boy was dressed, he padded after Dillon into the kitchen for their standard half pastry and a quick glass of juice. Calvin's day care served a light breakfast around midmorning, which meant Dillon didn't have to cook every morning.

"Will we see Moni today?" Calvin asked between bites of his pastry.

Dillon placed his glass of juice on the table. "I

don't know," he said carefully. "Do you want to see her?"

The boy nodded. "She smells good," he said. "Like Mama."

Dillon's heart contracted in his chest. At this moment, he hated Teena. "You've been thinking about your mom?"

Calvin nodded. "Moni smells like her. I like Moni."

Dillon didn't have a comment. He rubbed his hand lovingly across his son's head. "Finish your pastry so we can get to the center."

He was able to get Calvin out of the house and off to day care without mentioning Teena or Monique again. The knowledge that both women were on his son's mind as much as they were on his alarmed him. A boy Calvin's age shouldn't have to deal with a missing mother. And a man his age shouldn't have to deal with a lying ex-girlfriend from high school.

He turned his pickup onto Mondale Avenue and into the Elberton High parking lot. He and the principal had a nine o'clock meeting with the new curriculum specialist, Mrs. Monique Johnson Morgan. And he needed all the prep time he could get to put his emotions in check before seeing her. He knew they had a lot to talk about, but he wasn't ready to talk. He didn't think he could now. Not rationally, at least. And he didn't want their discussion to end in a shouting match. Monique was now a part of his life, whether he liked it or not, and they had to find a way to tolerate each other. For their son's benefit.

An hour or so later, Malcolm Thomas stuck his head in Dillon's office. "Monique's here," the principal said. "Our meeting has been changed to the library. She has some slides she wants to show us. See you in a few?"

"Sure," Dillon said, standing. Malcolm seemed awfully anxious to get to this meeting, he thought. Had Monique snared him, too? "I'll be along shortly."

"No rush," Malcolm said with a smile. "Ms. Morgan and I can spend some time getting better acquainted."

Dillon dropped back down in his chair as Malcolm closed the door. His suspicion had been right. Monique had, in fact, snared another male. Though this one was not a Bell, he was definitely her type. In his mid-forties, the still-fit Malcolm was just the kind of guy Monique would go for. If she was still into older men. Dillon knew for a fact that many a single woman in Elberton had set her sights on Malcolm. Unfortunately, not one had been able to capture the heart of the widower yet. At least, none before Monique.

But Monique had snared an older man before. She'd married one and given Dillon's son the man's name. How could she have been so uncaring of his feelings? he wondered again. Then she had the nerve to say she'd done what she did because she loved him. What kind of fool did she think he was?

Shaking off the negative thoughts, Dillon grabbed a legal pad and got up from his desk. He and Monique had a child together and they had to work together. While he would not have chosen to be in her presence as often as situations would force them to be together, he knew he could deal with it. All he had to do was learn to be around her without allowing his feelings—past or present—to get in the way.

He considered techniques for accomplishing this feat as he made his way to the library. At work, he'd treat her with utmost professionalism. If he was lucky, they wouldn't have to see each other except for casual passings in the halls and during weekly staff meetings. That shouldn't be too hard to handle. Though her role as the mother of his child and as someone Calvin had come to care about would mean more time spent with her, he figured he could handle the physical closeness by focusing on the boys and not on her. He could do anything for his boys.

By the time he walked through the library doors, he thought he had it all worked out. Until he heard her soft laughter. That sweet, tinkling sound stirred his memory and his emotions. He quickly tamped both down. What did she have to laugh about after the news she'd given him last night? he wondered, steeling himself against both his memories and his emotions.

Malcolm looked up and waved him over. "Glad you could join us," he said.

"Morning, Monique," he said smoothly.

She smiled, but he saw the uncertainty in her eyes. "Good morning," she said.

Malcolm clapped his hands together, oblivious to the undercurrents between Monique and Dillon. "Let's get started, then. Monique, you have the floor."

Monique stood up on wobbly legs. She could still feel Dillon's pain and his disgust. He hated her. He really hated her.

"Since we are getting started so late in the summer," she began, letting her skill at her job take over, "the curriculum analysis of the science department won't be complete until the end of the first six-week term."

For the next half hour she was a total professional as she told Dillon and Malcolm her plans. Malcolm asked appropriate questions to which she gave expert answers. This was her game and she was on. Dillon, on the other hand, was quiet. Too quiet.

"Good work, Monique," Malcolm said, again all smiles. "I think you have some innovative ideas that should help us tremendously." He turned to Dillon. "What do you think?"

Dillon didn't know what to think. He was sure her presentation had gone well, but he hadn't heard much of it. He hadn't been able to make his brain focus on Monique's presentation. As he sat looking at her in her pale pink suit, he couldn't get the picture of her, belly swollen with child—*his* child—out of his mind. And he couldn't get out of his mind the picture of the son they'd conceived together, either. The longer she'd talked, the more vivid the visions had become. And the more angry and hurt he'd become. The anger he accepted; the hurt he despised because it showed his weakness. His weakness for the first woman he'd loved. And Malcolm wanted to know what he thought of her presentation? "Good job," he finally said because it seemed most appropriate and least revealing. "I'm sure Monique can deliver everything she's promised."

"And we'll give her all the help she needs," Malcolm said. "I've been after the board of education to bring in a curriculum specialist for the last five years. We've got to make the best of this opportunity."

"What I'm going to need first," Monique interjected, "is some time with the staff."

Malcolm smiled again. "I'm way ahead of you there. Since the teachers will be in school the Wednesday, Thursday and Friday before Labor Day, I've scheduled sessions for you to meet with each department individually. Will two hours per department be sufficient?"

Monique nodded. "That'll be perfect."

Malcolm looked at Dillon. "I was thinking that you could sit in on the sessions with her, Dillon. To act as an intermediary of sorts and to show the staff that we're behind the work Monique is doing. Everyone needs to know she has our full support."

While Monique thought a school liaison was a good idea and would have suggested that one be named, she would never have chosen Dillon for the job. By the look on his face, she guessed he wasn't any happier with his new assignment than she was.

"Fine by me," Dillon said without a glance in her direction.

"Good," Malcolm said. He looked at his watch and got up. "I'm expecting a phone call. Why don't you two discuss the teacher sessions? When you're done, Monique, stop by my office and I'll take you to lunch as promised." He turned to Dillon. "You're welcome to join us, Dillon." Then Malcolm left without waiting for a response.

A thick silence fell over the room after Malcolm's departure. Dillon's eyes met Monique's and held her bound by the strength of his hatred. "I want to see him," he said.

She nodded. "Of course." There was so much to be said, but her tongue felt heavy in her mouth and she couldn't speak more than a couple of words.

"Does he know about me?" he asked, his eyes still brooding.

She nodded again. "Charles told him before he died."

His eyes widened in surprise. "So how long has he known?"

"Charles died three years ago. He told Glenn when he entered first grade."

"Did he understand?"

She stood up and went to the windows, looking out on the beautiful summer day. She rubbed her arms to ward off a chill that had nothing to do with the weather. "He was six years old, Dillon, and the father he loved was dying. He did his best."

"I'm his father." His words were harsh, but when she looked back at him his eyes were sad.

"I'm so sorry, Dillon. I thought I was doing the right thing."

"So you said." He refused to give her any quarter, though her sadness tempted him to do so. Deep inside, he knew that giving her a quarter would open him up to being hurt by her again and he wasn't about to do something that stupid. "Tell me again how you decided to give my son to another man because you loved me. I didn't quite get it the first time."

She dropped her arms in frustration. She wanted to scream, not at Dillon, but at the injustice in the world that had forced a teenage girl to have to make such a decision. And at the injustice that had separated her son from not one father, but two. And at the injustice that put the pain in Dillon's eyes today. "Do you really want to hear my explanation again, Dillon, or do you want an excuse to be angry with me and maybe even hurt me the way I hurt you?"

His gaze didn't waver, but he didn't speak for a long moment. When he finally spoke, his voice was soft. "Where is he?"

She sighed, then retook her seat at the table across from him. "He's at my sister-in-law's house in Charleston. I wanted to talk to you before I brought him here."

He fixed her with a hard stare. "What did you think I was going to do, Monique? Deny that he's my son? You really don't know me, do you?"

She shook her head again. "I was concerned about Glenn. I don't want him to be hurt any more than he's already been hurt. He's just a little boy, Dillon. I knew that you'd come around, but I didn't want Glenn exposed to the initial anger I knew you were going to feel, the anger that you're showing now."

Dillon jumped out of his chair. "What do you expect from me?" He thumped his chest. "I'm a man. A person with feelings. How do you think I feel knowing that the woman I loved more than life itself thought so little of my love that she chose to leave town pregnant with my child and marry another man rather than come to me? How the hell do you think it makes me feel knowing that I have another son out there? A son who may feel neglected and rejected just because you decided *you* knew what was best. You're damn right I'm angry. I'm angry with you for not being the girl—the woman—I thought you were, and I'm damned angry with myself for caring so much about you. Now when do we go see my son?"

She fought back the tears his words summoned. "We can go this weekend. I'll call my sister-in-law and tell her to expect us."

Dillon nodded. "Good." He picked up his pad from the table, and she knew he was going to leave.

"Dillon," she called.

He looked at her.

"Have you told your family?"

He cursed under his breath and ran his hand across his head. "No, and I don't look forward to doing so, either, but I'll tell them before we leave. And I'll have to tell Calvin, too."

She wanted to tell him again how sorry she was. She knew her news was turning his life upside down, but there was nothing she could do to stop the events her disclosure had set in motion. "How do you think Calvin will take the news? If you think it'll help, I'll go with you to tell him."

He gave her a derisive look. "What makes you think I'd want or need your help?"

Her head jerked back as if he'd slapped her. "I'm only trying to help, Dillon. This situation is not easy for me, either. And I know you have to be concerned about your son's reaction to the news."

Dillon dropped his pad back on the table and sat back down. He wiped his hands down his face. "This is a hell of a mess."

She sat down, too. "I'm sorry" was again on the tip of her tongue.

"Calvin has had so much loss in his life," Dillon began. "Too much for a boy his age. I thought he was about to turn a corner. But I really don't know how he's going to take the news that he has a brother."

"Maybe it'll be a good thing for both of them, Dillon. I know that Glenn needs you, needs his family. Maybe Calvin needs his brother. If we're lucky, both our boys will be better off knowing each other.''

He heard the hope in her voice and the concern. "How is Glenn—emotionally, I mean?"

"He's hurting, Dillon, and he doesn't know yet how to handle that hurt, so he acts up."

"How bad is he?"

"He's a good boy—don't get me wrong—but sometimes he just explodes. He's gotten into fights at school and he and I have had shouting matches." She looked away. Sometimes she felt that if she were a better mother, things with Glenn wouldn't have gotten so out of hand.

"Maybe that's good for him, Monique. It has to be better than the way Calvin holds things in. Sometimes I wish he would act out."

She nodded, one parent understanding another. "It's hard watching them hurt when you love them so much."

He didn't say anything; he didn't need to. In the silence that followed, he felt closer to her than he'd felt since she'd been back. The one thing they had in common was love for their sons.

Chapter Five

Later that afternoon, Monique signed a rental agreement for the large colonial near the school and the park. If things went well and she and Glenn decided to stay in Elberton longer, they could consider a more permanent arrangement.

Next, she drove to her apartment and called the moving company. Her furnishings and household goods—which had been in storage since their house sold a few months earlier—were scheduled to be delivered to Elberton in five days.

Needing to eat, but not wanting to order in as she usually did, Monique went to the Dinner Plate, the only restaurant in town that was open after dark.

A teenage waitress in a brown plaid shift with The Dinner Plate printed on the chest pocket greeted her with a smile and a large plastic menu. "Just one?" the perky teen asked. Monique nodded, and the girl scanned the almost-full room. After she spotted an empty table, she beckoned Monique to follow her.

Monique nodded to a few people whom she recognized, but she didn't stop to talk. She hadn't had that kind of friendship with the people of Elberton. Dillon had been her only friend. Just thinking about that made her remember the loneliness she'd felt before meeting him.

"This all right?" the girl asked, pointing to a booth just to the right of the salad bar.

"Perfect," Monique said, placing her shoulder bag on the plastic seat and sitting down next to it. The girl took her beverage order, told her to help herself to the salad bar, then sprinted away.

Monique let her eyes roam the salad bar. She wasn't really that hungry. She just hadn't wanted to be alone tonight. There were too many thoughts going around in her head and she needed to take a break from them. She knew she couldn't accomplish that by staying home alone. So here she was. She closed her eyes for a brief moment of rest before getting up to get herself some food.

"It's her." Monique heard the child's loud whisper. She opened her eyes and saw Dillon and Calvin on the other side of the salad bar.

"I told you it was her," Calvin said with a brief look up at his father.

Monique got up from her seat and joined them at the salad bar. "Hi, Calvin," she said. "I didn't think I'd see you here tonight."

"We come here a lot. Daddy doesn't like to cook much."

She glanced up at Dillon. There was no hint of a smile or of welcome in the look he gave her. She looked back down at Calvin. "I bet your dad is a really good cook."

Calvin turned up his nose. "Sometimes. Grandma is a good cook. Do you cook?"

Monique picked up one of the cold white dinner plates from the salad bar and fell into place behind Dillon, who was filling plates for himself and Calvin. "Sure I do. I like to cook."

"Do you have a little boy like me?" he asked innocently. "Is that why you cook?"

She looked up at Dillon, wondering if he'd told Calvin about Glenn. He shook his head slightly in answer to her unspoken question. "I have a little boy." *Just like you.*

Calvin's eyes widened. "What's his name?"

She glanced up at Dillon again. His face still held no emotion. "Glenn. His name is Glenn and he's in the fourth grade."

"Where is he?"

Kids and questions, Monique thought. Leave it to them to quickly get to the heart of any matter. "He's with his aunt."

"Is he coming here?"

Monique nodded. "I'll go get him in a couple of weeks. Right before school starts."

"He's going to school here? At my school?"

"That's enough questions, sport," Dillon said in a patient voice. "Monique wants to eat her dinner before it gets cold."

"Sorry," Calvin said, looking at Monique.

Monique couldn't resist touching a hand to the boy's smooth cheek. "That's all right, Calvin. You can ask me anything you want. But I'd better let you go eat your dinner now."

"Aw, okay," the boy mumbled.

Monique smiled up at Dillon. "See you later," she said, determined not to let Dillon's distance put a damper on her mood. She could have stayed home and moped. She turned away from the two males and went back to her booth.

A few seconds later, she looked up to see Calvin and Dillon standing before her. "We want to eat with you," Calvin said quickly. "Can we? Daddy said we could eat with you if you said it was okay."

Calvin was incorrigible, so like Glenn had been at his age. She smiled. "Of course I don't mind. I'd love for you to eat with me."

Calvin scrambled onto the seat across from her. Dillon placed their plates on the table then slid in next to his son. "I hope we aren't interrupting," he said. "But I figure we're going to have to get used to this."

Monique knew he was right, but she also knew he was uncomfortable sitting across from her. Maybe even as uncomfortable as she was sitting across from him.

"Do you have a husband?" came Calvin's question.

"Calvin," Dillon chastised. "What did I tell you about all the questions? Eat your dinner and stop asking so many questions."

The boy turned sad eyes up to his father. "I was just askin'."

"Well, stop asking and eat."

Calvin frowned, but he did as his father ordered. He picked up a French fry and pushed it into his mouth.

Monique met Dillon's gaze. "It's all right, Dillon. It really is. I don't mind answering his questions. Like you said, we may as well start getting used to it." She turned her attention to Calvin. "I was married, but my husband died."

"Was he sick?" Calvin asked, perking up quickly.

Monique nodded. "He was very sick."

"Did you and Glenn cry? Were you sad?"

Monique queried Dillon with a glance. After he nodded, she said, "Yes, we were very sad. We loved him, but we knew he had to go to a better place."

Calvin nodded as if he understood fully what Monique meant. He glanced over at his father. "Mama went to a better place, too. Didn't she, Daddy?"

Dillon cleared his throat. "Your mama's not dead, Calvin, you know that."

"But she went away and I was sad. Were you sad, too, Daddy?"

Anger better described what Dillon had felt when Teena left. Maybe he'd felt sadness, too, but not because she'd gone. No, any sadness he'd felt had been because her actions had shown how little regard she had for her son. "Yes, son, I was sad."

"But you didn't cry." Calvin made it sound like an accusation.

Dillon glanced at Monique before answering his son. "No," he said, "When your mother went away, I didn't cry."

Monique thought about the dinner conversation long after she'd said good-night to Dillon and Calvin. So Dillon's wife had left him and her son. Monique couldn't imagine what would drive a woman to leave her child. She laughed a sad laugh. As a child who'd been left behind herself, she knew exactly how Calvin felt. And she hated the woman who'd been so careless as to inflict that kind of pain on a child.

Monique determined then and there to do everything in her power to ease the pain she knew Calvin felt. While she knew she could never take his mother's place, she vowed to do what she could. He was such a wonderful little boy. Why couldn't his mother see that? Maybe, she thought to herself, Calvin and Dillon need me and Glenn as much as we need them.

As she let herself into her apartment and got ready for bed, she wondered about the woman Dillon had married. Had his heart been broken when she'd left him and Calvin? Did he still miss her? Did he want her back? So many questions she had, but no answers. And no right to ask for any. Not that the answers would matter. Calvin deserved better than the treatment his mother had given him, and Monique was going to see that he got it.

After she'd undressed and put on her nightclothes, she brushed her teeth and climbed into bed though it was only eight-thirty. She picked up her phone and dialed Sue's number.

Glenn answered.

"How's my boy?" she asked.

"When are you coming home, Mom?" Glenn asked.

Monique's heart quickened. She hadn't really thought he was going to miss her. Sometimes she felt so useless to him. "I'll be home this weekend. Guess what?"

"What?"

"I found us a house. You're going to love it,

Glenn. It has a big yard and a big tree with a tree house."

"I don't want to move," Glenn said. "I want to stay with Aunt Sue. I don't want to move."

"Glenn," Monique said patiently. "We've talked about this."

"I don't care. I'm not moving. I'm not moving."

"Glenn," Monique said in a raised voice, but it was no use. Glenn had left the phone. She heard mumbled words, which she assumed were coming from Sue and Glenn.

"He didn't mean that, Monique," Sue's exasperated voice said when she came on the line. "He had a rough day today."

Monique sat up straight in the bed. "What happened?"

Sue sighed. "Nothing really. Jonathan's father had promised to take Jonathan and Glenn out for pizza tonight, but he had to cancel because of work. Glenn didn't understand."

Monique heard Sue's words, but she also heard what Sue wasn't saying and she felt her son's pain. She thought about Calvin and how alike he and Glenn were. Two young boys in so much pain. "What am I going to do with him, Sue? What can I do?"

"You're doing what you can right now. You're making it possible for Glenn to know his father and the other half of his family. That's what he needs."

Monique knew Sue was right. She sighed. "I told Dillon last night."

"Last night? Why didn't you call me? How was it?"

"It was tough. He was angry. He still is. But he

wants to meet Glenn. We're coming up this weekend, if that's all right.''

"You know it's all right. This is what we wanted, remember? How are you doing, Monique? I know this has to be hard on you."

"I'm hanging in there." Barely, she added to herself.

"Stop being brave. This is me you're talking to. How are you really doing?"

How did she feel? Monique didn't really know. While she hated the anger that she felt coming from Dillon, she understood it and she accepted that she was going to have to live with it until he decided to let it go. "I'm happy, but anxious about his meeting Glenn. What if they don't get along?"

"So what if they don't? They will in time. Now, don't go looking for bad news."

Monique wondered if she were being naive about the entire situation. Could she really expect Glenn and Dillon to meet each other and immediately become friends as well as father and son? No, she knew she couldn't. They had a long road ahead of them. In time, she hoped they'd develop a father-son relationship or something pretty close.

"Dillon's wife left him and his son."

"Oh" was Sue's only response.

"It's been hard on Calvin. I don't think he's gotten over it yet. I don't know if he will. I didn't."

"You're wrong, Monique. You did get over it. You found out that you were loved and that you could love. You found out that your parents and your aunt were the ones who were wrong, not you. Calvin will do the same. You and Glenn will help him."

Monique pictured Calvin's sweet face in her mind.

"How do they do it? How do parents desert their children?"

"I don't know, Monique. At least Calvin was left with a loving father."

Monique knew that put the boy leagues ahead of her as a young child. Not only did Calvin have Dillon, he also had his grandparents and his uncles. All she'd had at his age was a spiteful and unloving aunt who never ceased to tell her how much of a burden she was. "Dillon is good with Calvin," she said. "They're really close."

"From what you've told me about Dillon, I know he has a big heart. A heart that can take in a couple more people to love."

"It doesn't matter about me, Sue," Monique said, refusing to entertain thoughts of being on the receiving end of Dillon's love again. "I just want him to have room for Glenn. Did he go to bed?"

"He's in his room, but I doubt he's asleep. Do you want me to try and get him on the phone?"

What Monique wanted was to be able to go into Glenn's room and hold him in her arms until he fell asleep. "Please do," she said. "I want to say goodnight to him."

While Monique waited for Sue to get Glenn to the phone, she thought about her aunt. The woman had moved out of Elberton a few years after Monique had left, and gone to live in a retirement community in Florida. She'd often talked about leaving Elberton, but Monique had been surprised to learn she'd actually done it.

She'd gotten in touch with the older woman once and tried to build a bridge for Glenn's sake, but her aunt was still as bitter as she'd been when Monique had left town. So Monique accepted that neither she nor her son were going to have a relationship with their only blood relative. That was sad, but for them it was also a fact of life.

"No, Darnell," Dillon said to his older brother. He'd called him and told him about Monique and Glenn right after he'd put Calvin to bed. After Darnell had expressed his opinion of Monique—which Dillon couldn't dispute—he offered to take the next plane to Elberton. "You don't have to come all the way home just because of this," Dillon said.

Darnell offered stiff resistance but Dillon was finally able to convince him not to make the trip. "Thanks, man," Dillon said. "You're not bad for a big brother."

Dillon hung up the phone with a much lighter load on his shoulders. He could always rely on his family's support. Sometimes they offered too much of it, but he didn't mind, because he'd come to count on them over the years. Even when they didn't agree with him, they stood with him.

And this would make the second time they'd had to stand with him as he fought his way through Monique's fallout. The first time he'd been a heartbroken boy, refusing to believe that she'd left him of her own free will. Sure, they tried to convince him that she'd gone just as her letter had said. But when they'd seen that he wasn't able to accept her letter as the end, they'd helped him find her. And when he'd come face-to-face with a married and pregnant Monique, they'd taken him back home and never murmured the words *I told you so*. They would never know how much he'd appreciated that consideration. Of course, as the years passed and he'd matured, they'd felt free to express their opinions vocally. But by then, he was emotionally able to handle it, so their words hadn't bothered him. Much.

He needed their support again tonight and he was sure he was going to get it. They were family, and he could count on them. Sure, his mother would fuss, his father might cuss and Donald would joke, but when it was over, they'd ask what he needed from them and when he told them, they would give it to him.

He had another son. Though he knew it was true because he had the pictures to prove it, he still couldn't believe it. Not really. And he wouldn't until he saw Glenn face-to-face, until he held him in his arms. This child born of the love he'd shared with the girl he'd thought he would grow old with. He'd been so young then. And so cocky. Maybe too cocky. He'd said he would love her forever and he'd meant it with everything that was in him. He'd loved Monique more than he could have imagined loving anybody. His love had made him go against his family. If she'd asked him to choose between them, there would have been no doubt that he would have chosen her. She'd been his heart.

And his heart had been ripped out when she'd left him. Now she was back, and she still had his heart in her hands.

A son. She'd given him a son. Somehow it seemed right that something tangible should have come from a love that was, for him, so powerful.

When he looked back on it now, he knew he and Monique had been too young to feel the emotions they'd felt for each other. He wondered how things would have turned out for them if they had met in college instead of in high school.

But they hadn't met in college. They met in high school, fell in love and separated. And now they were back together. Not in the way they had been, but back together just the same. Their son was the bond that would connect them forever.

He thought he heard a noise and went to check on his sleeping son. The night-light illuminated Calvin's face and showed that he was sleeping soundly. The love he felt for the boy in the bed was immeasurable. He hadn't known such a love could exist until he'd held the newborn Calvin in his arms. At that moment, his life had irrevocably changed. Every step he took, every decision he made, was made with Calvin in mind.

He'd been concerned about how Calvin would respond to the news that he had an older brother. Not surprisingly, when Dillon had given his son the news and told him about making the trip with Monique to see him, Calvin had expressed more concern about when and if his father was coming back than he had at the news that he had a big brother. Dillon understood fully the cause of his son's insecurity and he again cursed Teena.

Now he had a second son to consider. He eased Calvin's door shut and went back to the living room to await his parents and Donald. They knocked at the door before he was seated.

"What's wrong, Dillon?" his mother asked, leading the trio into the house. "Why couldn't you tell us over the phone? You aren't getting married to that girl, are you?"

Dillon raised his brows, causing his father and

brother to shrug their shoulders. "Who knows where she gets her ideas, boy," his father said, taking a seat on the couch next to his mother. Daniel and Katherine Bell were the perfect couple. Daniel, the stereotypical gruff and rough patriarch on the surface but a pushover underneath, was the perfect foil for the maternal and protective instincts of his wife.

"They're always together," his mother continued. "Harriet Jones told me they were at the Dinner Plate last night. Do you have to take her everywhere you go, Dillon? What are people going to think?"

Dillon shook his head, dropped down on the coffee table and faced his family. "I'm not getting married, Ma. You'd be the first to know if I were."

"Well, I would hope so," his mother said.

His father leaned forward and clasped his hands together. "Well, what did you want to talk to us about, son?"

"Yeah," Donald added. "Why'd you call us over here? I had to cut my date short. And the evening was just getting interesting."

"Donald!" his mother admonished.

"Aw, Ma," Donald said with a smile that Dillon knew had seduced many an unsuspecting woman. "I'm just teasing."

"Well, you can just stop teasing until we find out what your brother wants."

"Yes, ma'am," Donald said with fake contrition.

"Go on, Dillon," his mother said. "Tell us what it is you want to talk about."

Though he had considered many ways to break the news to his parents, right now direct seemed to be the best option. He took a deep breath. "Monique and I have a son. Together."

"What?" was his mother's response.

"A son?" was his father's.

"That was fast work!" was Donald's.

"What are you talking about, Dillon?" his mother asked. "How can you and Monique have a son? She's only been here a few days."

"Our son is nine years old. She was pregnant when she left town ten years ago."

"But I thought she was married."

"She was married," Dillon explained. "She got married *after* she found out she was pregnant. The boy is mine."

His father cleared his throat. "I hate to ask this, son, but how do you know for sure that the boy is yours?"

Dillon reached behind him and picked up the pictures he'd taken from Monique. He handed one to his mother and the other to his father.

"Well, I'll be," said his father.

"How could she?" asked his mother.

"I always knew you had it in you," said Donald.

Chapter Six

Dillon was glad he'd suggested they drive to Charleston. He felt it gave him some control in a situation that was, by the minute, proving itself to be totally out of control. Monique had suggested taking the short commuter flight, but he'd preferred the five-hour drive, thinking it would give him time to prepare himself. He was more nervous about meeting his son than he had been about going on his first date with Monique.

He glanced over at Monique. Her eyes were closed and her head lay against the headrest. He would have thought she was calm but for the constant thrumming of her fingers against the door handle. She was as nervous as he was. No matter his feelings about what she had done to him, he didn't doubt her love for her son. Their son. And that knowledge was beginning to make it difficult for him to keep his emotional distance. He and Monique had too much history. Too many good memories fought against the bad memories for space in his mind.

"Tell me some more about Glenn," Dillon asked, needing to direct his thoughts back to his son and away from Monique.

She stirred next to him and sat up straighter. "You don't want to get me started again. I can talk about him all day."

He gave her a small smile. "And I could listen all day. I'm his father, remember?"

She looked out the passenger window. "Of course I remember."

He knew she'd taken his remark as an attack, but he hadn't meant it that way. He'd only wanted her to know that he was as hungry for news about his son as she was eager to talk about him. "So tell me something," he encouraged.

She turned back to him with uncertain eyes. "He's a great boy, Dillon. He's just going through a rough time right now."

"Since your husband died, you mean?" The word *husband* was hard on his lips. He didn't like thinking of her as another man's wife.

"Since then, yes. He's become so needy, but it's not me he needs."

She made her last statement with such sadness that he wanted to reach out and touch her. "Let's hope it's me, then."

"I hope so, but he may be a hard case."

"I know," he said. "You've told me that already." And she had. She'd told him about Glenn's erratic behavior. His outbursts. The disconcerting way he handled disappointment. Again, Dillon thought that what was going on with Glenn was not much different than what was going on with Calvin. Both boys felt deserted. "He'll come around."

"What makes you so sure?" she asked.

"He's my son, isn't he?"

She laughed. The sound was a balm to his anxious heart. "He is that. When he's not being a holy terror, he's as sweet and even-tempered as I've always known you to be."

Her words made him remember the time when they'd been as close as any two people could be. She'd called him her sweet, sweet Dillon. He'd been embarrassed and a little bit insulted the first time she'd done so. But he'd soon come to cherish the words on her lips. They were her special endearment for him, and they never ceased to make his heart fill with love for her. He'd been so young back then. So young that her words could bring him to his knees with gratitude that she was his. That they were one.

Monique knew from Dillon's silence that he was remembering. Her words had triggered her memories, as well. "Sweet Dillon" she'd called him back then. The sweet boy who'd come into her dreary life like a knight on horseback. Her own personal savior.

She'd known what she was risking when they made love, but to her young mind the risk had been worth it. She'd been so needy for love, for companionship, that she would have done anything for Dillon. Not that he pressured her in any way. No, Dillon had always been the perfect gentleman. The first and only time they'd made love had been at her insistence. She'd had a terrible argument with her aunt and the older woman had said horrible things to her. When Dillon had picked her up for their date that night and she'd seen the love and caring in his eyes, she'd decided then that she needed him. She'd needed his love to wash away the hate that her aunt had poured over her.

Afterward Dillon had told her again how much he loved her and how he felt as though they were now married. But they hadn't been married. They'd been high school students in way above their heads. Way, way above their heads. That one time had been the only time they'd made love. But it had been enough.

"You know, Monique," Dillon said, interrupting her thoughts, "I love him even though I've never met him. And I have to believe that he's going to feel how much I love him and that'll make a difference."

She remembered how safe and secure she'd felt in Dillon's love. When he loved, he gave his all and it was a heady experience to be on the receiving end of his love. "It's made a difference with Calvin, hasn't it?"

He sighed. "I like to think so. Calvin's had a rough time, but together we're making it."

Monique wanted to ask why his wife had left him and Calvin, but she knew she didn't have the right. "He's a sweet boy. He reminds me a lot of Glenn at his age."

"Calvin's doing better, but I don't know if he'll ever get over his mother's desertion."

"Maybe he won't get over it, but he'll learn to deal with it." Monique spoke from experience. "Having somebody love you unconditionally makes a difference. It gives you strength." That was what your love did for me, she thought to herself.

"And loving him has given me strength. Because of my love for him, I can't afford to be weak. He needs me too much. I have to be strong for him. And now for Glenn."

"Thank you, Dillon," she said.

"For what?"

"For being strong. I know you haven't had much time to adjust to the idea of a son, and I know that you're still angry with me, but thank you for not holding any of that against Glenn."

"You thought I would do that?"

She considered his words so she could give him an honest answer. "I don't know what I thought. I just knew that Glenn needed you."

They drove the next few miles in silence as Dillon contemplated her words. "I know this is rehashing old territory, but why didn't you tell me you were pregnant, Monique?" he asked, a while later. "I deserved to know."

She looked at his profile. His jaw was tight and she knew it had cost him a lot to ask that question. Again. "I got scared."

"Scared? Of me?"

"Of your response. I lived with an aunt who spent every day of our life together telling me what a burden I was. I didn't want me and my baby to become a burden to you."

"But I loved you, Monique. And he was my baby, too."

He didn't understand and she didn't know how she could make him understand. But she had to try. "Think about how different your life would have been if you'd been saddled with a wife and baby before you even graduated from high school. Would you have gone to college? Would you be established in a career now?"

"We could have worked it out, but you didn't even give us a chance."

Monique had no defense. She'd done what she felt was best at the time. Now that she looked back on it, she knew she'd made the wrong decision. But she also knew that if she had to make the decision again, she would do the same thing.

"You're not my dad," Glenn shouted. He'd recently come in from a softball game and was dressed in his white uniform with red stripes. A red cap was turned backward on his head. "You're not my dad," he repeated, then he turned and ran out of the room.

"Glenn!" Monique and Sue called at the same time. Monique got up from the couch and followed the boy.

"Let me," Dillon suggested, taking hold of her arm. Seeing the question in her eyes, he added, "We have to start somewhere." He smiled to reassure her. "Where do you think he went?"

"There's a tree house out back. He's probably out there." There were tears in her eyes now. "Why do things have to be so difficult for him?"

Dillon gave in to his instincts and touched his hand to her cheek. "It'll be all right, Monique. He has two parents who love him very much. It'll be all right."

"Promise?" she asked with a feeble smile.

"Promise." He dropped his hand from her face and followed Glenn's path. When he reached the tree house, a wooden structure with four sides, a roof and an open doorway, he looked up and took a deep breath before beginning the short climb that would take him to his son's hideout.

When he reached the top rung, he saw Glenn sitting

against the back wall of the tree house. He called to him, "Is it okay if I come in?"

Silence.

"I just want to talk, Glenn. I promise to leave if you want me to leave."

"You're too big," came the muttered reply.

At least he was talking, Dillon thought. He was thankful for that. "What if I stay right here and we talk? This is a nice tree house you have. Did you build it?"

"Yeah."

"By yourself?"

"My *dad* helped me."

Dillon didn't miss Glenn's emphasis on the word, *dad*.

"Well, your dad did a good job. My dad built me a tree house when I was about your age."

Silence.

"But I had to share mine with two brothers."

"This one is mine all by myself. My dad said so."

Dillon figured his son was going to be a hard nut to crack. "You miss your dad, don't you?"

Silence.

"You want to hear about my brothers?"

Silence.

"Well, Darnell is the oldest. He drives a motorcycle. I bet you'd like him. Have you ever been on a motorcycle?"

Glenn moved away from the back wall of the tree house and closer to the door. "A real motorcycle?"

Dillon smiled. He'd known the motorcycle would get Glenn's attention. Not many nine-year-olds could resist a bike. "Yep. A real motorcycle."

"Does he let you ride it?"

Dillon shook his head. "Not me. I like cars. I feel safer on four wheels."

"I ride a bike. My mom gave it to me for Christmas. It has two wheels just like a motorcycle."

"Hmm," Dillon said. "Well, maybe Darnell will take you for a ride one day."

Silence.

"My other brother, Donald, is younger than me. He's a policeman."

"A policeman?" Glenn couldn't keep the excitement out of his voice. "Does he carry a gun and everything?"

"Sure does. A big gun, too."

"Does he shoot people?"

Dillon fought a smile. "No, he says his job is to keep from having to shoot people."

"But he'd shoot a bad guy, wouldn't he?"

"Only if he had to. Police don't want to shoot people. They'd rather talk people through their problems. Talking is better."

"Talking is dumb," Glenn said and Dillon heard the withdrawal in his words.

"Why do you say that?"

"People say a lot of things they don't mean. Talk, talk, talk."

Dillon's heart ached because of the disappointment his son had faced. "Sometimes people can't help it when things change. It's not that they don't mean what they say. It's just that things happen that they have no control over."

"Yeah," Glenn said with skepticism.

"So, how did the game go today?" Dillon asked. He could see that the other line of conversation was leading to a dead end.

Glenn lowered his head. "We lost."

"What was the score?"

"Eleven to ten."

"That was a close game. Your team must have played well. What position do you play?"

Glenn peeked up at him, but quickly dropped his eyes. "First base. I lost the game for us. I struck out. If I had hit the ball, the guy on base could have come in."

"You would have tied, but it doesn't mean you would have won."

"Well, at least I wouldn't have lost it for us."

Dillon wanted so much to touch his son, to comfort him, but he knew now wasn't the right time. "Well, that's one thing about sports. Sometimes you win. Other times you lose. The key thing is that you play your best. Did you play your best?"

Glenn nodded. "It didn't do no good. The guys were all mad at me."

"Maybe you need to practice your batting some more. If you want, I could help you."

Glenn lifted his head. At the neediness in the boy's wide expression, Dillon's stomach clenched. "You know how to play baseball?" Glenn asked.

"Sure. I was a pitcher. I still pitch on a summer team. I could throw you some, and you could practice your batting."

Glenn looked as if he was struggling. He wanted to accept the help, but he wasn't ready to be friendly with this man who said he was his father.

"Why don't you come on down from the tree house?" Dillon suggested. "We'll toss the ball around. If you decide you don't want to do it after a while, we can stop. What can it hurt? And it might help your game."

Dillon started down the ladder, hoping Glenn

would follow him. When he reached the bottom, he glanced up and saw Glenn looking down at him with a questioning frown on his face.

"Where's the ball?" Dillon asked.

Glenn hesitated, then turned around and went back into the tree house. He came out with two gloves, a ball and a bat. Dillon breathed a sigh of relief when his son started down the ladder.

"You're going to get a crick in your neck," Sue said from behind Monique. Sue had started preparing dinner even though Dillon had offered to take them all out to eat.

Monique turned from the window where she had been watching Dillon talk to Glenn. She'd breathed a sigh of relief when Glenn had followed Dillon down the ladder and they'd started tossing the baseball.

"So, how are they doing?" Sue asked.

Monique told her what she'd seen.

"Seems they're off to a good start," Sue observed. "How do you think Dillon feels about barbecue ribs?"

"Sure, Dillon eats ribs." Monique walked over to the stove and lifted the cover on one of the pots. "Want me to put some potatoes in the oven?"

"That'd be good."

Monique moved to the pantry and got the potatoes.

"So how are things between you and Dillon?"

"There are no *things* between me and Dillon. How many times do I have to tell you that?"

"Hmm."

Monique took the potatoes to the sink and began cleaning the dirt off of them. "What does 'Hmm' mean?"

"Nothing."

"Come on, Sue. Say what's on your mind."

"I've seen the way you look at him. You're still in love with him, Monique. Don't kid yourself."

"I'm not in love with him," Monique retorted. "Not really."

"And what's that supposed to mean?"

Monique turned off the faucet, turned around and leaned back against the sink. She didn't quite understand her own feelings, and if anybody could help, Sue could. "When I remember how we were together, how much he loved me, and how much I loved and needed him, yes, I can honestly say I do love him."

"But?"

Monique sighed. "But I'm not sure if I love a memory or if I love the man Dillon is now. Heck, I don't even know the man he is now."

Sue slid the ribs into the oven. "Maybe you know more about him than you give yourself credit for."

Monique couldn't think about Dillon, or look at him, without remembering the past, so she didn't see how Sue could be right. She told her so.

"Think about it, Monique. What do you know about the adult Dillon?"

"He loves his son, or I should say *sons*. And he seems to enjoy being with them. I saw it with him and Calvin, and now I see it with him and Glenn." She turned and gazed out the window at father and son again. "Right now, he seems to be having as much fun as Glenn."

"That's a good characteristic, I'd think," Sue said.

"Of course, it is," Monique answered. "Seeing him with the boys makes me want to love him."

"I sense there's another but."

"Yeah, I can't be in love with him just because he's good with his children."

"So, you're saying that you're not attracted to him?"

Monique turned away from the window again. "I wouldn't go that far," she hedged. She was most definitely attracted to Dillon. She wished she were free to touch him when she wanted.

"So he's a good father and you're attracted to him. What else does a good mate have to have?" Before Monique could answer, Sue added, "I know. What about his job situation? Is he a good provider?"

"I think so. He has a respectable job and he provides a home for him and Calvin." She considered for a moment, then said, "Yes, he's a good provider."

"Well, he's a good father, you're attracted to him and he's a good provider. That seems to me to cover the biggies. Unless you can think of something else?"

"Trust and love," she said softly. "Dillon no longer trusts me, and without trust, he can't love me."

Sue wiped her hands on a dishcloth, then went and pulled Monique into her arms. "Dillon still has strong feelings for you, Monique. He's fighting them right now, but he has them."

Monique accepted the comfort that Sue offered, but she didn't say anything. She couldn't afford to start thinking seriously about her and Dillon as a couple, as a family. No, she had to be realistic. She could dream about something that would never happen, but she would not allow herself to hope. She couldn't give the Fates another chance to snatch away her dreams.

Chapter Seven

Monique stood in the doorway of the den and watched her son and his father playing video games like two children.

"Gotcha, Dillon," Glenn said. "I'm killing you."

"Not yet," Dillon answered. "I can still get you."

"No, you can't."

"Yes, I can. Watch this!"

"Oh, no." Glenn fell back on the couch. "You got me."

Monique walked into the room. "And it's time for you to go to bed, young man."

Glenn turned to her. "Aw, Mom, we were just getting started. Do I have to go to bed now?"

"Yes, you do. You've already stayed up past your bedtime. It's almost ten o'clock. You should have been in bed right after your bath."

"Can't we play just one more game?"

Monique opened her mouth to deny her son's request, but Dillon spoke first. "Yeah, Mom, just one more game."

Glenn laughed and Monique propped her hands on her hips and put a frown on her face. "You're as bad as Glenn. No, no, no. Both of you need to get ready for bed."

Dillon laughed and ran his hand across Glenn's head. Monique's heart went soft with the casual exchange between father and son. "Say good-night, Glenn," he said.

"Good night, Glenn," the boy said, looking at Dillon. They both burst out laughing.

Dillon touched his son's head again, almost as if he couldn't help himself. "You'd better head for bed. Your mother doesn't think we're too funny."

Glenn looked up at Monique. "All right. Are you gonna be here tomorrow?" he asked Dillon.

Dillon nodded. "I'll be here all weekend. We'll practice your hitting again tomorrow, okay?"

"Okay. I'll see you in the morning."

"Night, Glenn."

"Night, Dillon."

"Night, Mom."

Monique stopped Glenn as he was about to pass her to leave the room. "Aren't you going to give your old mom a hug?"

Glenn sneaked a peek back at Dillon, who wisely turned his head. Glenn turned back to Monique and gave her a quick hug. "Night, Mom," he said again.

"Night, sweetheart. Sleep well."

With that, Glenn shot out of the room.

"He certainly has a lot of energy." Dillon slumped

onto the sofa and yawned. "If you hadn't sent him to bed, I think I would have gone to sleep on him."

Monique sat on the love seat across from him. "Your room's ready if you want to go to bed."

He sat up straighter. "I'd like to talk for a while if you don't mind."

She shook her head. "I don't mind. I wanted to talk, too. I think today went pretty well, don't you?"

"It's a decent start," Dillon said with a nod. "He's not ready for another father just yet, but I think he can accept another friend."

Monique nodded. "I noticed he called you Dillon. How do you feel about that?"

A wry smile crossed his face. "Of course, I wish he'd call me Daddy, but I can wait on that. It'll come in time. He's a good boy, Monique. You've done a great job with him."

"Thank you," she said, enjoying his praise. "Sue's been a lot of help."

"She's quite a woman. How does she feel about all this?"

She knew he referred to his being Glenn's natural father. "It's never been a secret in our family, Dillon. Charles knew and she knows. She only wants what's best for Glenn." Monique didn't think she should tell him about Sue's expectations of a romantic relationship between the two of them.

"Aren't you gonna miss her when you move back to Elberton?" he asked.

She folded her legs under her. "That's why I'm trying to convince her to come with us. So far, she's not going for it."

"I like her."

"I'll be sure to tell her. She likes you, too. She

thinks, and I agree with her, that you're good for Glenn."

Dillon took a deep breath. "I know I've given you a hard time for not telling me about Glenn when you first found out you were pregnant. But I want you to know that I appreciate your telling me now. I realize that you didn't have to."

Monique's throat felt full. "I did it for Glenn," she said. "He needs you and he needs your family. They're his family, too."

"And they can't wait to meet him. I had to bribe Ma to make her stay home this weekend. She wanted to come see her grandson."

Monique wished she could have been a fly on the wall when Dillon had told his family. "I bet they had some not-so-nice things to say about me."

"They were concerned."

Monique chuckled. "You don't have to be nice, Dillon. I know your parents never liked me."

Dillon studied her, as if measuring what to say to her. "They didn't really know you. But I think they'll like the woman you've become."

The piercing look he gave her almost made her squirm. "What's with you, Dillon? Why are you being so nice to me all of a sudden? Did Sue put something in your water tonight?"

Dillon stood up, walked over and sat next to her on the love seat. "I guess I deserve your skepticism. But in spite of everything you've done, Monique, you're a good mother. You're good with Glenn and you're good with Calvin. When my folks see that side of you, their opinion of you will change. I'm sure."

Monique decided she liked the angry Dillon much better than the tender, sweet one before her now. The angry one she could resist; the sweet one endangered her heart. She looked away from him. "It doesn't matter."

He placed his finger on her chin and turned her face toward him. "It does matter. We're going to be spending a lot of time together and the boys don't need to feel any tension between us."

She should have known his words were for the boys' sakes. But she admitted she'd hoped Dillon was reacting and speaking out of feelings he had for her. "You're right. They don't need to feel any friction. Are you going to be able to keep a lid on the anger you feel toward me?"

He smiled, a deep smile, the first real one he'd given her. "When I see Glenn, I can't be angry. I love him, Monique, and like I said, you didn't have to tell me about him. I'm honestly grateful for that. So I'll try to concentrate on my gratitude for your finally telling me the truth, rather than my anger at your lying to me ten years ago. There's nothing either of us can do to change the past anyway."

They were silent after Dillon's statement and Monique felt a closeness to him that frightened her. He was being so sweet and he was so close. If he wanted to kiss her, he'd only have to move his head a few inches.

She dropped her gaze and broke the spell. What on earth had she been thinking anyway? Dillon had just finished telling her that his only concern was for the boys. And here she was going all goo-goo over him. She just hoped he hadn't seen the longing that she was sure was in her eyes.

He moved away from her and stood. "I guess I'll head for bed. Night, Monique."

She met his gaze again and thought for a brief second that she saw longing in his eyes, too. Her imagination must be working overtime. "Night, Dillon."

As Dillon prepared to go downstairs for breakfast the next morning, he tried to get his thoughts off of what had happened between him and Monique last night. Yes, something had happened. Though neither of them had said anything, something had happened between them. Had she been any other woman and had history been different, he would have kissed her last night. Hell, he would have kissed her in spite of their history if she'd shown him the slightest encouragement.

But she hadn't. And that was probably a good thing. He and Monique didn't need to start something that they could never finish. It was best that they keep their focus on the boys.

When he got downstairs, Sue and Glenn were already in the kitchen. "Morning," Dillon said, wondering where Monique was. She didn't strike him as the type to sleep late. He wondered if their incident last night had her avoiding him. The notion did not sit well with him.

"Hi, Dillon," Glenn said. "Are we still gonna practice batting today?"

Dillon shot his son a bright smile, though his heart ached with the youngster's insecurity. "Of course, slugger, I told you we would."

"Morning, Dillon," Sue said. "What can I get you for breakfast?" She rattled off a long list of dishes.

"What are you trying to do?" he asked. "Fatten me up?"

Sue laughed. "Hardly. But if you're going to keep

up with Glenn, you're going to need your strength. Isn't that right, Glenn?"

"Get the waffles," Glenn said. "Aunt Sue makes the best waffles in the world."

Dillon smiled. "Okay, I'll go with Glenn's recommendation, but only on one condition." He pointed a finger at Sue. "You have to let me take us all out to dinner tonight. I don't like the idea of you cooking for me every day."

"But—"

"No buts," Dillon said, extending his hand to confirm the deal. "Do we have a deal or not?"

She smiled and shook his hand. "We have a deal."

"What kind of deal?" Monique asked, entering the kitchen through the back door.

"I just offered to take you all to dinner tonight and Sue agreed," Dillon answered, his eyes taking in the picture she made in her multicolored culottes and tank top. She looked young and without a care in the world. He liked the look.

"Actually he twisted my arm," Sue clarified, setting a plate of waffles in front of Dillon.

"They're ganging up on me, Glenn," he said, leaning toward his son. "Aren't you going to help me?"

Glenn looked from his aunt to his mother. "They're bigger," he quipped.

Dillon, Sue and Monique laughed, and Dillon realized how much he loved Monique's laughter and the relaxed expression it put on her face. His stomach muscles tightened.

"I think I need Calvin here to help me."

Silence ruled the room.

"Who's Calvin?" Glenn asked innocently.

He's your brother, Dillon wanted to say. "He's my four-year-old son."

Glenn slipped a piece of waffle in his mouth. "Does he live with you?"

"Sure does. We live in a house with a big yard and a big wide porch."

Glenn seemed to think about that for a minute or two. "Does Calvin play baseball?" he asked.

Dillon sighed. "He plays, but he's not as good as you are. He's just a little guy and he needs a lot of practice."

Glenn took a sip from his juice glass. "Well, maybe I could help him since I can play real good."

"Really well, Glenn," Monique corrected.

Glenn rolled his eyes. "I can play really well. I could teach him how to run and how to catch and how to throw. And you—" he looked at Dillon "—can help us with our hitting."

Dillon caught Monique's glance and would have bet that there were tears in her eyes. He was kinda choked up himself. "I think that's a great idea, Glenn, and I know Calvin will think so, too. What if we all go to the Braves game next weekend?"

"Oh, boy, a Braves game." Glenn looked at Monique. "Can I go, Mom, can I?"

"Sure, you can go. Maybe I want to go, too."

Glenn shook his head. "No, you're a girl. This is just for guys, right, Dillon?"

Dillon fought back a grin. "Well, I don't know. If your mother and aunt really want to go..."

"They don't. They can go shopping or something."

"Glenn!"

"Aw, Mom, you know you and Aunt Sue like to go shopping. Men like to go to ball games."

Monique looked at Sue. "Do you get the feeling we're not wanted?"

Sue smiled. "Sorta, but I really don't mind. I kinda like shopping."

Dillon laughed at the betrayed expression that crossed Monique's face at Sue's comment. He was looking forward to next weekend already.

Monique walked into the den just as Dillon was hanging up from his daily call to Calvin. While she wanted to talk with him about his day with Glenn, she was concerned about the closeness they'd shared last night. She wouldn't admit to herself whether she was concerned that they would share the same closeness and more tonight or that they wouldn't.

"How is he?" Monique asked. She knew about the calls, and wished she could speak to the little boy. A part of her was disappointed because Calvin hadn't asked to speak with her.

"He's fine. He asked about you."

She smiled. At least he'd asked about her. "That's good. I miss him, you know."

He smiled too. "You hardly know him, Monique. How can you miss him?"

"You missed Glenn before you even met him," she accused.

"That's different. Glenn's my flesh and blood. We're connected."

She shrugged, then sat down on the couch and hugged a pillow to herself. "I know I haven't known Calvin long, but I still miss him. He's such a sweet little boy." She felt connected to Calvin because of the similarities in their lives, but she wasn't ready to discuss those similarities with Dillon yet. "Did you tell him about the ball game next weekend?"

He nodded. "And he's as excited as Glenn was.

You don't mind about the game, do you? I know I didn't check with you first."

She put the pillow aside. "Of course I don't mind, Dillon. It's a wonderful idea and I'm glad you thought of it."

"Even though you aren't invited to the game?" He smiled.

"I'm a little hurt that my own son is a chauvinist, but I'll let it slide this time."

Dillon laughed, then got up from his seat at the desk and walked over to sit next to her on the couch. His manly scent filled her senses. "We had a good time today," he said. "I think Glenn likes me."

"I know he does," Monique said, wishing there was some way for her to move away from Dillon without bringing attention to herself. With him this close to her, she couldn't stop thinking about their almost-kiss last night. "You're so good for him, Dillon." *But you're nothing but trouble for me.*

"Don't get overly confident, Monique. We still have a long way to go."

"Oh, I know." She moved the pillow between her and Dillon. She tried to be casual in her motions, but the smile that played at Dillon's lips made her wonder. "It's just that now I feel we're going to make it. Before, I wasn't so sure."

"What changed your mind?"

She shrugged. "I don't know. You. Glenn. Us."

"Us?"

Had he moved closer? It was as if she could feel his breath on her neck. "Yes, us. We're getting along and the boys need that."

"All of this is for the boys, right?"

"That's right," she said.

Dillon had known he was in trouble as soon as he

moved from the desk and sat next to her on the couch. He'd known and he hadn't cared. He was just curious. Curiosity couldn't hurt, could it? He pushed away all thoughts of cats.

"Haven't you wondered, though?"

"Wondered what?" she asked, not meeting his eyes.

"Wondered if it would be the same?"

"What? No."

He moved closer. "I can't stop thinking about last night," he whispered. "I've tried, but I can't stop thinking about how it would feel to kiss you again."

She licked her lips. Dillon wondered if she even realized she was doing so. "Kiss me?"

He rubbed his finger down her cheek. "One kiss," he said. "What would one kiss hurt?" He looked into her eyes and saw the banked passion...and the welcome.

She leaned slightly closer to him. "I'm not sure."

"Why don't we try it and see?"

Before she could answer, he brushed her lips with his own. He'd always thought she had the softest, sweetest lips and she still did. He couldn't help himself. He increased the pressure on her lips, teasing and tasting.

She moaned deep in her throat and parted her lips slightly. That was all it took. He immediately dipped his tongue in and tasted the inside of her mouth, sampling to see if and how she'd changed. He pulled her into the circle of his arms.

Monique knew one or both of them would regret the kiss as soon as it was over, but she didn't let that stop her from enjoying the moment. She'd wanted to be in Dillon's arms since she'd first seen him that day at the school. It was only now that she let herself admit how she'd longed for him ever since the day she'd walked out of his life.

She'd left him, but she'd left her heart with him. She'd always belonged only to him. And though she knew there was no future for them, not really, she accepted this moment in time as her due. She'd waited ten years to have him hold her, and she was going to enjoy it. She gave more to the kiss, trying to take enough to sustain her for the rest of her life.

Soon, too soon, he pulled away. She saw the confusion in his eyes and waited for his words of regret.

Dillon didn't know what had happened between them. He just knew that he loved the feel of Monique in his arms. It was almost as if she'd never left him. When he held her, he could almost believe she loved him. Almost.

"That wasn't bad," he said, making the understatement of the year. That kiss had rocked him to the point that he wouldn't be able to get up from the couch without embarrassing himself.

She wouldn't meet his gaze. "No, it wasn't bad. At least, now we know." She stood and brushed her hand needlessly across her head. "I guess I'd better go to bed."

"I guess you'd better."

He watched her as she left the room, head held high, shoulders straight. His Monique. She was right about one thing: At least they knew. And God help them what they did with the knowledge.

Chapter Eight

Monique covertly observed Dillon out of the corner of her eyes. She so loved watching him with one of the boys. It didn't matter if it was Glenn or Calvin. She just loved seeing him love. And he did love both boys unconditionally. She didn't have to guess about that.

But this afternoon as she watched him tussle with Calvin on the green grass of Elberton Park, she was thinking about the kiss they'd shared yesterday in Charleston. The kiss that had kept her awake more than half the night and had all but robbed her of an appetite this morning. The sly looks from Sue had indicated her sister-in-law had some idea what had gone on last night with Dillon. Monique was glad that Glenn had seemed oblivious to the tension flaring between her and Dillon.

At least she and Dillon knew, she repeated in her

mind. She'd already known that she still loved him and found him attractive. What she hadn't known was how much she still wanted him. And how much he obviously still wanted her. While knowing the latter appealed to her feminine vanity, the practical side of her knew the knowledge only placed her in jeopardy. She harbored no illusions that Dillon still cared for her, and she wanted—no, needed—more than the physical relief she would find in his arms.

Just because she and Dillon were getting along amicably didn't mean he'd forgiven her. Not by a long shot. She still wasn't sure he believed her when she told him she'd done what she had because she loved him. She wondered if she would believe a story like that if she were in his shoes.

She sighed and directed her attention to two little girls playing patty-cake. No use thinking about her and Dillon. Better to think about Dillon, Glenn and Calvin. She wanted so much for their relationship to work. Glenn needed the stability and the roots that Dillon could give him. She just hoped her son would accept the love that Dillon had to give him. And if things worked the way she wanted them to, Calvin would be the beneficiary of a large dose of love himself. She had so much in her heart to give him.

Calvin chose that moment to run over to her. "Did you see that, Moni?" he asked, almost out of breath. "I had Daddy down on the ground and he couldn't get up."

Monique smiled then touched the boy's cheeks. She'd gotten used to expressing her affection, and found herself doing so at every opportunity. He seemed to enjoy it as much as she did. "Why, sure I saw you. For a while there, I thought I might have to come help your dad out."

The boy laughed, an open, carefree laugh that made Monique think all was right with the world. "You're a girl. You couldn't help Daddy."

Monique looked up when Dillon laughed.

"I didn't know chauvinism was in the genes, Dillon, but it must be since Calvin and Glenn both seem to have their share." He grinned at her and her stomach got all fluttery. She wanted him to kiss her again. She wanted to be held in those big, strong arms and have those big, tender hands touch her all over. She cleared her throat. "You're just as bad as they are."

"Now I didn't say a thing. Don't go getting mad with me."

She looked at Calvin. "But he was thinking it, wasn't he, Calvin?"

The little boy looked from one to the other and shrugged. He really didn't know what she was talking about.

"Let's go get some ice cream," he suggested.

Monique looked to Dillon for direction. "Sounds good to me," he said. "How about you, Monique?"

"I've got to stop hanging out with you guys or I'm going to be as big as a house. I think I've already gained a pound or two."

"I doubt that," Dillon said. "But if you have, you've gained them in all the right places."

She turned and met his gaze. A mistake. His look was full of masculine appraisal and appreciation. While flattering, she didn't need his compliments today. Not when her resistance was at such a low level. She wondered what Dillon was doing anyway, tossing compliments her way.

"Well, just don't look too closely," she said. "You might see more than you want to see."

He lifted a brow as if challenged by her statement, and she wondered again what kind of game he was playing. She tore her gaze away from him and took Calvin's hand for the walk to the ice-cream shop.

During the short walk, Calvin asked, "If Glenn is my brother, does that make you my mother?"

The question took Monique by surprise. She looked to Dillon for an answer. He stopped and stooped down so he was at eye level with Calvin. "You know that Teena is your mother, Calvin. Why would you ask that question?"

The little boy tightened his grip on Monique's hand and shrugged. "Dunno," he said.

Dillon glanced up at Monique before inquiring further. "I think you do. You can tell me, Calvin. I'm not upset with you and neither is Moni."

Monique stooped down to join them. "Your father's right, Calvin. You can tell us."

He lifted his big brown eyes to Monique and said softly, "I like you. You'd be a good mama. You live here."

Monique's heart turned over with love for the little boy who had become so dear to her. She followed her instincts and gathered him in her arms. "Oh, sweetie, I like you, too. I'd love it so much if you were my little boy. You know that, don't you?"

She felt his little arms wrap tight around her neck and she had to close her eyes to keep her tears at bay. When she opened them, Dillon was staring at her with a curious look on his face. She couldn't tell if he was angry, happy or confused. He reached out and caressed his son's back and Calvin turned to include him in the embrace. Monique's only regret was that Glenn wasn't with them to share this special moment.

Dillon told himself that he had everything under control. He was attracted to Monique. That was no big deal. She was an attractive woman, and he was a living and breathing man. There was nothing abnormal about his response to her as an attractive woman.

It was the emotions he felt now as they held Calvin in their arms that were abnormal. And the emotions he'd felt when the two of them had discussed the problems with Glenn. Those were the emotions that scared him. Those emotions made him remember the good times between them. Those emotions made dents in the barriers around his heart. Those emotions made the "what if" questions loud in his mind. *What if* Monique had made her choices because she loved him? *What if* the two of them were able to find what they'd once had?

He shook off the questions. There was no use asking questions that had no answers. His best bet was to spend his time and his energy fighting his emotions. In order to do so, he knew he would have to be a lot stronger than he'd been last weekend when he'd kissed her. He tried not to think about the kiss, but he didn't seem able to stop. Every time he looked at her, he remembered how good she'd felt and how open she'd been. He'd tried to tell himself that she was as good at faking emotions now as she had been when they were in high school. But that tack lost meaning when he saw her with her arms wrapped around Calvin and tears of love and caring in her eyes.

She was a wonderful mother—there was no getting

around that fact. He admired what she'd done with Glenn and the inroads she was making with Calvin. Monique was the perfect mother, as perfect as he'd always known she would be.

He wondered what kind of wife she'd been, but he couldn't wonder very long because he didn't like thinking of her as another man's wife. He knew he had no right to feel proprietary where she was concerned, but he did. He only hoped that soon he would get over the feeling.

Kissing her like you did last weekend is not going to help you get over it, a voice inside his head warned him. And he knew the voice was right. That kiss had been a big mistake. He'd kissed her to take care of his curiosity. Well, he'd taken care of it, all right. He was no longer curious about kissing her. Now, he wondered if making love to her could possibly be as sweet as it had been the one time they'd made love before. He didn't think he should follow that curiosity to its logical end, though.

Dillon ceased his musings as Calvin twisted out of the group hug and said, "Are we gonna get ice cream?"

He smiled, then glanced over his son's head at Monique. "Are you ready?"

She wiped at her eyes with her fingers, then nodded. "I think I could use a nice, cold treat."

"Let's go, then."

They stood together, and each taking hold of one of Calvin's hands, they walked to the ice-cream shop in comfortable silence. Once there, they ate their cones at one of the white concrete tables outside the shop. When Calvin finished his, he headed off to the playground equipment. Dillon and Monique watched him, enjoying his happiness.

"He's taking the news well," Monique observed.

Dillon sighed. "So far, so good. This weekend will be the big test."

"Are you worried about it?"

He shrugged. "Not worried. More like anxious for this to be over and Glenn to be here. I miss him."

His words warmed Monique's heart. "He told me you called him. He was very excited about it."

Dillon grinned. "Well, I don't want him to forget me."

"Not on your life. And he can't wait to meet Donald, the policeman, and Darnell, who owns the motorcycle. You really pulled out all the stops."

He grinned again. "He was being such a hard case. I had to do something, or we would have spent the entire weekend in a silent war." He sobered. "He's really a good kid. If I haven't told you enough, you've done a great job with him."

Dillon's praise meant a lot to Monique. Being a mother was the most important thing in her life. "He can be difficult at times. But you've seen a glimpse of that."

"He misses Charles," he said. "Will you tell me about him?"

Monique wasn't sure if he was talking about Charles, the father, or Charles, the husband. She decided to talk about Charles, the father. "He was good to Glenn. From the day Glenn was born, Charles treated him as if he were his own son. They were inseparable." Sadness returned as she remembered Charles getting sicker. "Even as his illness progressed, he still made time for Glenn. They built the tree house when Charles was at his worst. But somehow he managed it. For Glenn. Watching him with Glenn made me realize just how much I had missed as a child—that unconditional love. I don't remember ever feeling that kind of parental love."

Monique was silent as memories of the past filled her heart. She was glad, so very glad, that Glenn had never experienced the pain of a loveless home. She'd spared him that at least. And she would have done anything to spare him Charles's death. But there was no way she could have known that Charles would leave them so quickly.

"You loved him a lot, didn't you?"

She knew that Dillon was now talking about Charles, the husband. "Yes, I loved him. But it was more complicated than that."

Dillon shook his head. "Love doesn't have to be complicated. You loved him. There's no sin in that. I'm glad you were happy. You deserved to be."

She looked at him with skeptical eyes, not believing the words he'd spoken. "You don't really mean that, do you?"

He touched his hand to her jaw. "It hurt when you left me. God, how it hurt. And I've hated you for the way things ended for us. But I've always wanted you to be happy. If he made you happy, then I'm happy for you. You can't help who you love. Or, in our case, who you don't love." He dropped his hand and turned his attention back to Calvin.

Monique wanted to tell him that the love she shared with Charles in no way diminished the love she had—would always have—for him, but somehow the moment passed. She wondered if she'd ever be able to tell him the entire story and have him believe her.

* * *

After putting Calvin to bed for the night, Dillon grabbed the latest Easy Rawlins mystery in an attempt to pass the time. He knew it would be a long time before he fell asleep because he couldn't stop thinking about tomorrow when Calvin and Glenn met each other for the first time. He figured Saturday and Sunday would be okay because they had plans, but Friday night was causing him some concern. It was important for both boys that the night go well.

He was concerned about Monique, too. It was becoming more and more difficult to keep his distance with her. It was as if she was burrowing a hole through the armor he had placed around his heart. And he didn't like it. He had been on the receiving end of pain two times too many to think about trying again with her.

Then why did you kiss her? his conscience asked. Dillon sighed, rubbed his eyes and tried to concentrate on Easy's problems.

"What you reading, bro?"

Donald's voice surprised him and he almost dropped his book. "What the heck are you doing, Donald? Why didn't you knock?"

Donald gave his brother a lazy grin then slid down on the couch. "You shouldn't have given me a key if you didn't want me to use it."

"That key is for emergencies. It's not for every time you get the urge to drop in. I ought to take it back."

"Won't do you any good," Donald said, getting up from the couch. "I made a copy." He went into the kitchen and Dillon could hear him rumbling around in the refrigerator. "You've got to start stocking the brew. Real men drink beer, or haven't you heard?"

Dillon didn't bother to reply to the beer comments. Donald knew very well that he didn't keep beer in the house because of Calvin. "Why don't you go home and drink your own beer? This is not a bar."

Donald came back into the living room with a can of orange juice. "I'm just a little dry." He popped the tab on the can and flicked it into the ashtray as he took his seat on the couch again. "What are you so grouchy about anyway? Having problems with your woman?"

"I don't have a woman."

"Ahh." Donald gulped the juice as if it were beer. "That could be your problem."

Dillon closed his book and slapped it on the coffee table next to the ashtray that held the flip-top tab from Donald's juice can. "Right now, you're the only problem I have."

Donald placed his can on the coffee table. "Really, what's wrong, man? You're wound tight as a drum. Something must be on your mind. Come on. What is it? Monique? The boys? Both? Tell me."

Dillon sighed then slouched back in his chair. "I'm taking Calvin to meet Glenn tomorrow and I'm a little worried about how they're going to react to each other."

"They'll be fine. Look at us. You didn't like me the first time you saw me, and now I'm your favorite brother."

Dillon laughed. "Yeah, right." He and his brothers had had their differences, their fights even, but they'd always stuck together against the world. The Bell

Brothers. One for all and all for one, just like the Three Musketeers.

"Well, I certainly don't believe that Darnell is your favorite. He's the one who got you to put your head in the toilet."

Dillon laughed again. Darnell had definitely filled his role as older brother. He'd tricked him and Donald into doing some stupid things. To this day, it was hard for Dillon to believe they'd been so gullible. "Darnell had a mean streak."

"You're telling me. I'm the one who sat in the closet all night trying to get a picture of Santa Claus. Boy, it was dark in there, and I was scared to death."

"You were more stupid than I was."

Donald shook his head. "No, I was just younger. I could blame my naiveté on age. You, on the other hand, should have known better."

"We had some good times when we were kids, didn't we?"

"Sure we did. If you don't count the fights, the yelling and the getting in trouble."

"That was part of the fun." Dillon thought about the young lives of Calvin and Glenn. "I wish Calvin and Glenn could have had as simple a childhood as we had. We were lucky. We had parents who loved each other—and us—and we had each other."

Donald clapped his brother's shoulder. "Calvin and Glenn are lucky, too, Dillon. They have you, and me, and Darnell and Ma and Dad, and Monique. They'll be all right."

Dillon had told himself much the same thing, but it was good hearing it from another person. "When did you get to be such an authority on children and families?"

"Hey, I read a lot."

"Are you sure you don't have a special lady somewhere and you're thinking about becoming a one-woman man?"

"I'm already a one-woman man."

"Humph."

Donald grinned. "You've never seen me with more than one woman at a time."

"You know that's not what I meant."

"Yeah, I know. But I'm not thinking about settling down yet. I haven't found the right woman." He wiggled his eyebrows. "I'm gonna keep looking, though. Yeah, even it takes the next fifty years, I'm gonna keep right on looking."

Dillon shook his head. One day some woman was going to come along and knock his brother on his behind. Dillon wanted to be there for that event.

"What about you?" Donald asked.

"What about what?"

"You thinking about settling down again?"

Dillon immediately thought of Monique and quickly pushed the thought aside. "I've got enough on my hands with the boys. A wife would be a bit much to handle."

"Oh, I don't know. A wife could help with the boys." He paused and took another swig of juice. "Especially if she cared about them as much as you do."

Dillon couldn't imagine being with a woman who didn't love his boys as much as he did. But right now he could only think of one woman who fit that bill, and she was definitely out of the question. "If you find such a woman, you let me know."

"I've already found her," Donald said.

"Who?"

"Don't play dumb, Dillon, you know I'm talking about Monique. She's Glenn's mother and Calvin's crazy about her. I bet she loves them as much as you do."

"Monique is out of the question," Dillon asserted.

"Why?"

"You know why. That woman doesn't handle the truth very well. I couldn't be in a serious relationship with a woman I couldn't trust, and I can't trust Monique. If the going got tough, I couldn't count on her to hang in there with me. No, Monique is not the one."

Donald turned his juice can up and drained its contents into his mouth. "It's your life, brother, but remember you only have one."

Chapter Nine

"Night, boys," Monique said. She and Dillon stood in the doorway of Glenn's room at Sue's house.

"Night, Mom."

"Night, Moni."

"Sleep well, men," Dillon added. "We have a full day ahead of us tomorrow."

"All right, Daddy."

"Okay, Dillon."

Dillon switched off the overhead light and closed the bedroom door, leaving the boys in darkness punctuated only by a slight night-light next to the bunk beds Sue had bought for Glenn.

"You sleepy?" Glenn asked from the top bunk.

Calvin stifled a yawn. "You?"

"Not me."

"Me neither," Calvin said, wanting to be like his older brother.

"Have you been to a Braves game before?" Glenn asked the younger boy. He'd never been to a professional game himself.

"No, but I watched one on TV with Daddy." He didn't add that he'd fallen asleep before the game was over.

"I've never been, either. My dad was gonna take me, but he got sick."

"Did your daddy go away?" Calvin asked.

"Yeah, something like that," Glenn said, not wanting to scare the younger boy with talk of death. He was probably too young to understand anyway. Calvin was still a baby.

"My mom went away, too."

Glenn wasn't quite sure what Calvin meant. "Where'd she go?" he asked, not wanting to ask if his mother was dead like his dad.

"I dunno. My daddy said she had to go away so she could be happy."

"Oh," Glenn said, wondering why Calvin's mother couldn't be happy at home.

"Glenn?" Calvin called.

"Yeah."

"Are you my big brother?"

Glenn paused for a minute. Dillon had said he was his dad, but his dad was dead. Still, Glenn didn't want to hurt the little kid's feelings. "I guess I am."

Calvin smiled. "I'm glad."

Glenn smiled, too. "I guess I'm glad, too. I've never had a brother before."

"My daddy has two brothers. A big brother and a little brother. And now I have a big brother."

"And I have a little brother."

"Are you really gonna show me how to play baseball?"

"Sure, I'll show you. Dillon has been helping me."

Calvin yawned again. "Glenn?"

"Yeah."

"I'm sleepy."

Glenn yawned, as well. "Me, too. Go to sleep."

"Night, big brother."

"Night, little brother."

Monique folded her legs under herself and waited for Dillon to join her for their evaluation of the evening. She thought the boys had gotten along well. There had been a little tension in the air at first, but once Sue suggested Glenn show Calvin his tree house, things had been set in motion.

"I was hoping you'd still be up," Dillon said. He was fresh from the shower and looking good enough to eat in his clean jeans and white golf shirt. More than anything, she wanted to move next to him and inhale his masculine cleanliness. "I had to wash off some of the grime. It takes a lot of energy to keep up with those boys."

"I thought you did pretty well."

He dropped down on the couch next to her. "But I felt it. I'm not as young as I used to be."

She smiled. "None of us are."

He studied her and she felt his masculine approval. "You don't look too worse for the wear."

"Thanks, I think."

"Hey, it was a compliment. You look good. But you don't need me to tell you that. I bet you have your share of admirers."

Actually, she didn't, but she didn't see any need to correct Dillon's assumption.

"I'd wondered about that."

"Wondered about what?" she asked, distracted by his closeness.

"Whether you had a man in your life. Your husband's been dead for three years now. I would think that you would have gotten remarried."

She shook her head. "I've been too busy with work and Glenn to think about getting married. What about you? Your wife's been gone a long time."

"Ouch," he said. "You don't give a guy a break, do you?"

"What did I do?" she asked, not understanding his problem with her question. "You asked me the same question."

He eyed her as if weighing the truth of her words. She hated that he still examined everything she said before accepting it as truth. "I guess I did."

"You still haven't answered my question."

"About marriage?" He shook his head. "I'm not interested in getting married again. One time was enough."

"Ah, that just means that you haven't found the right woman yet."

He shook his head again. "No, it means that I'm not interested in getting married. I have Calvin and now Glenn and that's enough for me. More than enough."

He must have loved his wife a great deal to not even want to consider remarriage, she thought. She wondered again why Teena had left him and Calvin.

"Go ahead and ask."

She looked up at him. "Ask what?"

"Ask why she left. I can tell you're dying to know. You're still transparent in some areas."

She didn't bother to deny it. "Okay, why'd she leave?"

"Same reason you left," he said, causing her to wince. "She wanted a more exciting life than I could give her here in Elberton. Seemed I picked the wrong woman twice. I don't think I'll be going down that road again."

Monique knew that was what she had told him in her letter, but that hadn't been how she'd felt. She'd wanted to build a life with Dillon wherever he wanted to go. "Everything I said in that letter was a lie, Dillon. I just made up some stuff so you wouldn't come after me and find out that I was pregnant."

"But I did come after you and I did find out."

"And I lied again."

"You didn't lie about everything. You were married and you were pregnant." He could still see the slight swelling that had been her stomach. Just as he could see the man who had held her hand—a man old enough to be her father. "And you seemed very happy."

In fact, she'd been miserable. No, that wasn't exactly true. She'd missed Dillon horribly and hated not telling him the truth, but she'd felt that marrying Charles had been a new lease on life for her. Sure, Charles was helping her out by marrying her and taking care of her and her baby. But their relationship hadn't been one-sided. He'd needed her as much as she'd needed him. They'd started with a business arrangement that had grown into a very dear friendship, but it had never been more than that. Of course, Dillon didn't know that, and somehow telling him now would make light of what she'd shared with Charles.

"Charles was good to me," she said.

"I bet he was. An older guy with a pretty young thing like you. And pregnant, too. His friends all probably thought he was some stud."

She felt the anger in Dillon's words and hated that the relaxed evening she'd expected was not to be. "Charles wasn't like that."

"Then tell me what he was like."

"He was a good man," she began slowly. "I met him in the restaurant where I was able to find a job. He was a regular and we became friends. I told him I was pregnant and he said he wanted to help me."

"Just like that?"

She got up and went to the windows. It was dark out and she couldn't see, but she needed to put some distance between her and Dillon. "When it's right, you know it." She was thinking as much about her and Dillon as she was about her and Charles.

Dillon got up and stood behind her. She could feel him, though he didn't touch her. "I know what you mean," he whispered.

She turned around. He was standing too close. "Don't," she pleaded, as vulnerable to him as he was to her. But she knew she wanted more from him than he wanted from her. He wanted her body, but she wanted all of him.

"I can't help myself," he murmured as his eyes caressed her. "I can't get that kiss out of my mind. Every time I look at you, I think about it. I don't want to. God knows, I don't want to, but I don't seem to be able to help myself. You've always had that effect on me."

He lowered his head then and she didn't move away from him. She couldn't. She still loved him. And wanted him. She moaned when his lips pressed against hers. It was a soft kiss, almost as if a feather had been brushed across her face. He placed his hands on her waist, and she relaxed against him. She could handle soft caresses like this.

He lifted his head suddenly and looked down into her eyes. The leashed passion glittering in his dark eyes challenged her, and she began to wonder if she'd let her guard down too soon. She couldn't handle the passion she saw in his eyes. She knew she should run—in her head she knew it—but her weak heart, putty in his hands, knew only that he was her love.

When he lowered his head again, she wrapped her arms around his neck and pressed closer to him. Her senses were on alert and sirens were going off in her head, but she ignored them all. It had been ten years. Ten long years. And she deserved this. She deserved him.

With his lips still glued to hers, he lifted her in his arms and took her back to the couch, easing her down on the soft cushions. The warning bells sounded louder, but it was no use. She was no longer capable of stopping.

Dillon's hands shook as he caressed her cheek. He wanted her so much. He remembered the time when he'd looked forward to being free to make love to her every day, many times a day. Thoughts of the long life of loving they would have together had made it possible for him not to touch her when they were dating. Except for that one time. That one night when she'd asked him to love her. She'd felt in his arms that night the way she felt tonight. Open and loving.

He knew his mind was playing tricks on him. Monique didn't have those kinds of feelings about him. Glenn was the reason she was back in his life. Had her husband lived, he never would have seen her again. Never have known his son.

That knowledge made him angry, but not angry enough to let her go. Just angry enough to make him despise his weakness for her. What was it about this woman that had captivated him so?

He kept his eyes closed as he trailed his finger down her cheek to her neck and down to her chest. He hesitated before allowing his hand to undo the top button of her shirt. Then he lowered his head and placed a kiss along her breastbone. What was going to happen between them was a done deal. There was no need to hurry.

"Daddy, you still up?"

Calvin's words quickly brought Dillon to a standing position.

"Calvin," Dillon said as Monique struggled to right her clothes.

Calvin walked around the sofa and looked between the two of them. "Were you and Moni wrestling?"

Dillon cleared his throat. "No. What are you doing out of bed?"

Calvin looked between the two of them again. "I had to go to the bathroom and then I wanted some water. Will you get me some water?"

"Sure," he said to his son, then looked over the boy's head at Monique. Her face wore a look of relief. He believed that same look was on his face, though he admitted he was a bit disappointed that they hadn't finished what they'd started.

"I'd better go to bed," Monique said quickly. "I'll

see you two in the morning." With that she fled up the stairs.

Dillon looked down at Calvin. The boy had kept him from making a grave mistake, he was sure of it. "Now, let's get you that water so both of us can get to bed."

Dillon and Monique managed to avoid eye contact the next morning over breakfast. Monique was glad he was taking the boys out. If he were to hang around the house all day, he would surely figure out that she'd been up half the night thinking about what had almost happened between them.

"I guess we're off," Dillon said after the boys had finished breakfast and gotten dressed for the game. "Sure you two don't want to come with us?" he asked her and Sue.

"Not me," they both said.

Sue laughed, then added, "I don't want to horn in where I'm not wanted."

Monique rubbed one hand across Glenn's head and the other across Calvin's jaw. "You guys have fun. I want to hear all about the game when you get back."

"Okay, Mom."

"Okay, Moni."

Dillon met her gaze. "We should be back before it gets dark. Should I feed them before I bring them home?"

Monique looked at the two boys. "I have a feeling they're going to load up on junk food at the game. Just have a good time."

"Okay, then, I guess we'll be going." He sounded as if he didn't want to leave, but she knew that didn't make sense. She'd better watch it. Now she was reading romantic motivations into the man's every move.

"I guess you'd better."

"Yeah, come on, Dillon."

"Come on, Daddy."

Dillon allowed the boys to pull him out the front door. Monique and Sue laughed as they watched them pile into the car and drive off.

"He's wonderful with the boys," Sue said.

Monique kept staring at the driveway. "He sure is."

"Couldn't find a better father than Dillon."

"Hmm. You're right."

"Good father, good husband."

Monique turned to Sue then. "Not again."

"Yes, again. Stop fighting it, Monique."

Monique began to clear the breakfast dishes. "Fight what? I'm not fighting."

"Oh, yes you are. You're fighting your feelings for Dillon. You're both fighting."

"Yeah, well, maybe that's because we know it's no good. It has nowhere to go."

Sue shrugged. "Who says it has to go anywhere? You're both young, attractive people. Can't you just enjoy each other without thinking of fifty years from now?"

"It's not that easy."

Sue directed Monique to sit in a chair at the table. "I know it's not easy. That's why you have to do it. You've been running since I've met you. Now's the time to stop running and face your feelings, Monique. Give yourself and Dillon a chance."

"But what if it doesn't work out?"

"There are no guarantees, sweetheart. But at least

you'll know. You won't have all these questions in your mind and you'll be free to look elsewhere."

Monique wasn't sure she wanted to do as Sue suggested. For so long the love she'd shared with Dillon had been hidden in her heart and cherished. If she tried again with him and failed, she would not only lose him, she would also lose the memories that had sustained her for a major part of her life. She wasn't sure she could risk losing that security blanket. "I'll think about it" was the best answer she could give Sue.

"Well, you just do that. But you'd better think about it soon. The sexual undercurrent between you and Dillon is so thick that you can cut it with a knife. It's going to be resolved one way or the other, and I'd hate for that way to be in bed before either of you are ready."

Monique didn't deny Sue's words. What happened last night was proof that what she said was true. In spite of all that lay unresolved between them, the sexual attraction between her and Dillon was very strong. "How did I get myself in this situation?" she asked herself, though she spoke the question aloud.

"Life, sweetheart. You live it, you make mistakes, you learn. And if you're lucky, you get a chance to make right some of the mistakes. You're one of the lucky ones."

Chapter Ten

As Monique sat watching Dillon, Glenn and Calvin line up against the formidable team of Donald and Mr. Bell in the Bell version of Labor Day football, her heart pounded in her chest. How easy it was to dream of a future together when she saw Dillon with the boys the way he was today. How easy it was to think of her and Dillon as loving parents.

Fortunately for her, reality always seemed to intrude on those dreams. There was no use in getting her hopes up, only to have them dashed later. What she and Dillon shared was sexual attraction. Very strong sexual attraction. Their actions two nights ago in Charleston made any attempt to pretend otherwise useless.

They'd successfully avoided being alone since their aborted lovemaking attempt. But, to Monique's dismay, the avoidance only seemed to enhance the attraction. Every time she heard his voice or saw his face, she remembered how it had felt to be in his arms. And she remembered how much she'd wanted him. How much she still wanted him. Knowing her feelings were reciprocated didn't make the situation any easier to tolerate. No, the passion in Dillon's eyes when he looked at her, the caress in his voice when he spoke to her and the seduction in the ever-so-casual touch of his skin against hers raised her temperature so high that she felt as though she were at the equator.

She forced her gaze away from the man-play and turned to offer her help to Dillon's mother. Again. The older woman had twice refused her, but Monique felt obliged to keep trying. Not only did she want to help with the picnic fixings, she also wanted to form some type of truce with her son's grandmother.

She drew in a deep breath, alighted from the redwood picnic table and walked over to the grill where Mrs. Bell had taken over for her husband. "I'd really like to help," she offered for the third time.

"You've done more than enough," came Mrs. Bell's terse reply. It didn't take a genius to figure out that the woman's response wasn't in reference to the food or the picnic.

Monique took a quick glance back at the men. Seeing that they were still thoroughly engaged in their game, she decided to discuss the problem that lay between her and Dillon's mother. "I know you don't like me much, Mrs. Bell," she began.

"You haven't been very likable," the older woman said.

Monique sighed. "I know."

The older woman looked up, surprised. She studied

Monique's face for something—Monique wasn't sure what—then she asked, "How could you do this to him? Glenn's his son, for God's sake."

Monique didn't know how she could explain the situation to Mrs. Bell and make her understand when she hadn't even been able to accomplish that feat with Dillon. Yet she felt a need to try. "You remember how I was back then," she began, remembering herself. She'd been tough and distant. So much so that before she and Dillon had become friends, she'd spent a great deal of time in detention and had garnered a reputation around town as a troublemaker. "I was a confused and scared teenager. Can't you put yourself in my position for at least a minute?"

Monique ignored the answer in the woman's silence and continued. "I was seventeen years old, pregnant, scared to death, living in a house with an aunt who hated me, in love with a boy whose parents despised me. I wanted my baby more than anything and I wanted Dillon, but I didn't want to be a burden to him. Don't you understand?" The look in the older woman's eyes said she didn't. "Just think what Dillon's life would have been like had I told him I was pregnant. What do you think he would have done?"

Mrs. Bell looked away. "He would have wanted to marry you and take care of his child," she said softly and Monique knew the words had been hard for her to speak.

"And what would have happened if we'd gotten married? Do you think Dillon would have gone to college? Do you think he'd be vice principal at the high school now? Do you?"

"So you did this for Dillon?" the older woman questioned with skepticism.

Monique smiled sadly. "For him, for me and for the baby. If Dillon had given up his dreams because of me and the baby, he would have come to resent us. And I couldn't have borne seeing his love for me die under the strain of some overwhelming sense of responsibility. I couldn't bear for him to look at me and our child as burdens who'd ruined his life. I couldn't do it."

The older woman didn't say anything, nor did she look at Monique again. She just focused her attention on the grill. Tired, frustrated and near tears, Monique turned away from her, berating herself for thinking she could make some dent in the woman's feelings for her.

"Hand me the platter on the table, will you?" Mrs. Bell said, not turning around.

Hope welled up in Monique's heart as she reached for the platter and handed it to Dillon's mother. "Here you go," she said.

"Thanks," came the sincere-sounding reply. "Why don't you pull out the paper plates and cups and pour everybody something to drink? I think it's about time to eat."

Monique stared at the older woman's back, and the unfamiliar urge to hug Mrs. Bell close rose up in her. She fought the impulse and turned and set the picnic table as instructed. Mrs. Bell hadn't exactly welcomed her into the family with open arms, but she'd extended a hand. Monique gladly took it.

Dillon settled down on the same side of the picnic table as Monique with Glenn and Calvin sitting between them. His mother and father and Donald sat across from them. Only Darnell's absence kept the day from being complete. Darnell had called with some emergency and had vowed to visit his new nephew as soon as he could.

But Dillon couldn't really complain. He was happy. Or, rather, as happy as he'd been in a long while. He was a family man at heart, and right now he felt family as he'd never felt it before. This day, this setting, was straight out of his dreams. Him, Monique, their kids, his family—all together and all happy.

He glanced over the heads of the boys who chattered incessantly about any and everything and observed the woman who'd walked back into his life and given him so much pain yet so much more joy. Whatever pain her reappearance had caused was more than compensated for by the joy of knowing and being with Glenn, his son.

Dillon turned his gaze from Monique. As he did so, his eyes locked with his mother's. She wore a reserved smile as if she, too, was happy, but worried at the same time. He didn't have to ask what troubled her. And while he wished he could tell her not to fret, that everything was under control, he couldn't lie to her. Nothing was under control. Even now his body pulsed with a need unlike any he'd felt in years. A need for Monique.

Her laughter brought him out of his musings.

"Do that again, Uncle Donald," Glenn was saying.

Calvin chimed in right behind his big brother. Dillon couldn't have wished for the boys to get along better. Calvin had found an instant hero and leader in Glenn, while Glenn had easily fallen into the role of the sage older brother.

Dillon looked across the picnic table at his brother balancing a plastic spoon on his nose. He shook his head at the childishness of his brother's antics, but he also laughed.

"Can you do that, Dillon?" Glenn asked.

"Yeah, can you do that, Daddy?"

"I'm not sure I can top that," he said, ignoring the pain he felt that Glenn still called him by his first name. He knew it was too soon to expect the boy to accept him totally. But it hurt him that his oldest son readily accepted his uncle Donald and his grandpa and grandma.

"Mom can do it. Can't you, Mom?" Glenn asked an obviously embarrassed Monique. Color flamed in her cheeks and her eyes grew bright. "She's done it lots of times. Do it, Mom."

"Come on, Monique," Dillon encouraged. "Let's see you do it." The image of this woman playing the clown for the child she loved so dearly only served to make him want her more.

"Maybe another time," she said.

"Aww, Mom," Glenn said.

"Hey, fellas," Donald interrupted, with a wink and a smile for Monique. "What are you trying to do? Have a girl show me up? I told you we men have to stick together. Right?"

"Right," both boys said.

Mrs. Bell clapped Donald on his shoulder with a serving spoon. "You're a bad boy, Donald Bell."

Donald grinned his take-no-prisoners grin, and Dillon couldn't help noticing the smile that crossed Monique's face when he did so. "It's in my blood, Ma. Don't blame me. Blame Dad."

Daniel Bell lifted both hands. "Don't bring me into this. I've always been a good boy." He hugged his wife's shoulders and lightly kissed her lips in a show of affection that was normal for them. "Why do you think Santa brought me the best gift in the world?"

Donald and Dillon both groaned at their father's loving playfulness. "Don't you two get started," Donald said. "Remember the young eyes we have here."

The older Bell shushed Donald and kissed his wife again. Dillon smiled and looked at the boys who were smiling, as well. When he lifted his glance to Monique, he was surprised to find yearning in her eyes. As if she sensed him looking at her, she turned her head ever so slightly in his direction. When their gazes met, it was a case of spontaneous combustion. He could feel her in his arms. Responsive. Ready. Willing. And he wanted to make that feeling a reality.

There was no use denying anymore what had happened between them two nights ago at Sue's house. He'd tried to tell himself that it was just a case of heightened emotions. But now he knew that wasn't true. Hell, he'd known then it wasn't true. He just hadn't wanted to face the truth of his feelings for Monique.

The truth was that she had cast some spell over him and he was totally unable to resist her. He found himself in a constant state of wanting. But for the presence of the boys—and he hated that he used his children as shields—they would have already taken this…whatever it was…to bed and figured out if they could conquer it.

His mother said something that caused Monique to reluctantly tug her gaze away from his. But the broken spell didn't change his raging emotions. He and Monique needed to talk about what had happened between them and stop acting like a couple of teenagers.

They were adults. Surely they could handle their emotions in an adult fashion. All they had to do was sit down and talk things through.

So what if he were attracted to Monique? he asked himself. That didn't mean he had to follow through on the attraction. He returned his attention to his food, praying he was strong enough to fight what he felt.

"And don't give Donald any trouble," Monique told Glenn who was eager to head off to the ice-cream shop with Uncle Donald. The three adults and two children had been watching the Elberton Labor Day fireworks from the elder Bells' back porch.

"Aww, all right, Mom," Glenn said.

"That goes for you too, Calvin," Dillon added. He then turned to Donald. "Do *not* let them talk you into allowing them to get on the playground equipment. It's late and they need to be getting ready for bed instead of going out for ice cream. What made you suggest that anyway?"

Donald merely grinned at his brother. "Hey, I just wanted some time alone with my nephews. I'll bring them back safely. You two worry too much."

"Wait until you're a parent," Monique said. "Then you'll understand."

"That'll be a long wait," Donald said, pulling the boys to him. "Let's go, fellas. I'm ready for some ice cream."

"Yay," the boys chorused.

Monique looked at Dillon who came and sat down next to her. The two of them shared a smile. "At least they're getting along," she said.

"They are at that. I didn't realize there would be a downside though."

"Downside?" she asked.

The streetlights illuminated his face when he grinned. "Yeah. They get along so well that they gang up on us. Reminds me of some other brothers I know."

She smiled. "You, Donald and Darnell."

"There wasn't a trick in the book that we didn't pull. And Darnell was the leader, since he was the oldest. He always had some gimmick, and like little robots Donald and I went along with everything he said."

Monique envied the childhood that Dillon spoke of, much as she'd envied it when they were teenagers. She'd never felt the love or the camaraderie that he shared with his brothers. And she'd often wondered what it must be like. Even though she'd never personally experienced it, she was glad that her son would. She'd brought him to Elberton so he could. "The boys are loving it. And I think Glenn loves having an uncle. He's needed men in his life for a long time, and he's just taking all of you in, including your dad."

"And Ma," Dillon added in a wistful tone that Monique didn't expect.

"What is it, Dillon?" she asked. "Aren't you glad he's accepted them so easily?"

He stood up and extended his hand to her. "Walk with me," he said.

Responding to the sudden change in his demeanor, Monique took his hand. "What's wrong?"

He led her down the steps, around the house and out onto the sidewalk. The street was filled with the sounds of laughter, music and families just having a good time.

"Are you going to tell me what's bothering you?"

"Glenn calls Donald, Uncle Donald."

Monique squeezed his hand. He was concerned about his son's affection. "He'll come around, Dillon. It's just easier for him to accept Donald as an uncle than it is for him to accept you as a father. I know he enjoys being with you, and he's starting to count on you to be there for him."

"I certainly hope so."

"Well, I know so," Monique said with confidence. "I think he may feel that accepting you as a father would somehow be disloyal to Charles."

Dillon looked down at her, and the concern and love in his eyes touched her deeply. "Has he said anything?"

She shook her head and wanted to press her palm against his cheek in an act of comfort. She resisted the urge. "If he says something, I'll let you know. But I think we should just let things take their course. They're moving along as well as we could have expected."

He didn't respond immediately, and she knew he was considering her words. "I know you're right," he said with a sigh as they turned the corner. "I never expected to feel this way. It's as though I'm jealous of the affection he shows Donald, and that makes no sense."

She stopped, and when he stopped, too, she looked up into his eyes. "That's so sweet, Dillon."

"Oh, no," he said with an exaggerated sigh. "Not sweet again."

She smiled. "Yes, sweet, dear and normal."

He shook his head. "Normal to be jealous because

your son calls his uncle Uncle? Doesn't sound normal to me."

"That's because you expect so much of yourself." And of those around you, she added silently. "It's only human that you want your son to call you Daddy. It's like when they're babies and you want their first words to be Mama or Daddy. Glenn's first words were Uncle, and you wanted them to be Daddy. It's perfectly normal that you're disappointed."

He did what she'd been too hesitant to do—he placed his hand against her cheek. "How'd you get so smart?"

"Nine years with Glenn," she said softly. Her heart beat so heavily in her chest that she wondered if he heard it. His hand against her cheek burned into her soul.

He chuckled. "That'll do it, all right." He dropped his hand from her face, took her hand in his and continued walking.

Monique tried to keep her traitorous thoughts on Glenn and Calvin, but they wouldn't obey. Instead, they entertained visions of her and Dillon as they had been before, and teased her with what they could possibly be again.

"Did you enjoy the day?" he asked.

She'd more than enjoyed it, but she didn't want to let him know how much. "I'm glad the boys had a good time."

"That's not what I asked."

She sucked in a deep breath. "I know."

He stopped again and looked down at her. This time the passion of the other evening was back with them and she knew they were on the road to trouble.

"I had a very good time," she said. "Your family was very gracious to me."

"Hmm." He stared at her lips and she hoped he wasn't thinking the same thing she was thinking. "I told you they'd like you."

She couldn't help it. She ran her tongue across her lips. She'd had to. With him staring at her as he was doing, her lips had felt dry and brittle. "I wouldn't say that they like me yet, but we're moving in that direction."

"And what direction are *we* moving in, Monique?" His voice was a soft caress.

She opened her mouth to deny they were moving in any direction, but he lowered his head and captured her mouth with his, and all thoughts of anything but the kiss fled her mind. She'd wanted to kiss him this way since that ill-fated lovemaking attempt at Sue's house. It was only a kiss, she told herself as she leaned into him, responding to his attack on her senses.

Dillon heard her moan in the back of her throat and increased the pressure of the kiss. It had only been two days, but it seemed ages since he'd held her in his arms. He'd tried denying his longings, and when that had failed, he'd tried ignoring them. Obviously, that wasn't working, either.

It's just a kiss, he told himself, but he knew he was lying. This wasn't just a kiss. It was a heart-scorching display of passion on a sidewalk in plain view of anyone who happened to walk by, drive by or look out of their windows.

He took one last nip at her lips, then regrettably lifted his head. Seeing the question in her eyes, he couldn't resist the temptation for one more nip. He took it, then smiled at her.

"What are we doing?" she asked, breathless from his kiss, but needing to know what he wanted from her.

"Seems to me that we're kissing in the middle of the street," he said.

She dropped her gaze from him and started walking again. "That's not exactly what I meant."

He fell into step with her. "I know what you meant. And I'm not sure what we're doing."

Though she'd repeatedly told herself not to expect anything, she was hurt by his evasive answer. "Whatever it is, I think it needs to stop."

Dillon didn't respond. He didn't want to think about what was happening between them. He knew that if he thought about it, he would come to the conclusion she'd just voiced. It needed to stop. It needed to stop because there was no future for them. Not with the history they'd shared. "You're right," he said with more confidence than he felt. "And I'm sorry for getting carried away. It won't happen again."

"Good," she said, but could say no more. Her heart had clogged up her throat. Why did it hurt so much that he didn't put up more resistance to her suggestion? Why couldn't he have expressed some modicum of care for her? Why? Why? Why?

Chapter Eleven

Monique was still asking herself "Why?" the next day as she rushed through her meetings at the high school, so she could squeeze in some time to meet Glenn's new teacher at Elberton Elementary before he started classes on Friday. She wanted to be sure his teacher understood that she was going to be an involved parent.

At the end of her third session, she checked her watch and realized that she was almost late for her eleven o'clock teacher meeting. She ran by her office, dropped off some papers and quickly headed for the door.

"Hey, where are you rushing off to?" Malcolm asked. He and Dillon stood in the hallway outside the principal's office near the front entrance of the school.

She smiled, sparing only a brief glance at Dillon. Though they'd agreed that the kisses they'd shared would not be repeated, she couldn't forget or dismiss the attraction she had for him. "I'm running late for a meeting with my son's teacher," she told them.

"Why didn't you mention this to me?" Dillon asked.

She gave him a full appraisal then. And he looked most attractive in his casual dark brown suit. He also looked angry. "It didn't occur to me, Dillon," she answered honestly.

His look said he didn't believe her. He turned to Malcolm. "Can we finish talking about this later? It seems I have a meeting at the elementary school."

Malcolm nodded, though Monique noticed the curious expression that came across his face. He obviously wondered what was going on with the two of them.

Dillon took Monique's arm and escorted her out of the building and in the direction of his pickup. "My car's over there," she said, pointing in the opposite direction.

"And my truck's over here." He pointed to the red pickup. When they reached it, he opened the passenger door. "Get in. I'll drive."

"This is not necessary, Dillon. I can drive."

He ushered her into the truck, ignoring her words. "No need for us to take two cars." He closed the door, a bit forcefully in her opinion, then strode around to the driver's side and got in.

She tried not to be offended by his high-handed manner since she knew he was upset.

"If you want me to be a part of Glenn's life," he said once he was in the truck, "then why are you shutting me out of the important things?" His words were an accusation.

"I'm not shutting you out. It simply slipped my mind, Dillon."

"Like it slipped your mind when you found out you were pregnant?"

She winced. "That's not fair and it's not true. This was an honest mistake. Back then, I deliberately kept the truth from you."

Dillon knew he was overreacting, but he'd been overreacting all morning. First, he and Calvin had an argument about whether Calvin should go to day care or stay at his grandmother's with Glenn. In the end, they'd decided that Calvin would stay at his grandmother's with Glenn until Glenn's school started. Then he'd had an argument with Malcolm about some inconsequential matter. And now this problem with Monique. She probably *had* forgotten to mention the teacher meeting to him. Hell, she'd been Glenn's sole caretaker, other than some help from Sue, for the last three years, and she was used to being solely responsible for him. "Well, I'd appreciate it if we could talk about these things. I want to be a father to him, Monique, but you're going to have to help me."

"I know, Dillon, and I want you to be a father to him. I'm sorry I didn't tell you about the meeting with Mrs. Edwards, but, like I said, it didn't occur to me."

He believed her. And if he'd gotten any sleep last night, he would have seen the truth in her words immediately. "Okay, and I'm sorry for coming on so strong. I've been having a bad morning." He didn't see any need to tell her about his lack of sleep or the fact that it had been her face in his mind that had kept him awake.

"Don't worry about it," she said, wondering if the cause of his bad morning was the same as the cause of her hectic one. She was doing anything and everything to keep from thinking about the kisses they'd shared.

He cast her a quick glance. "So are you planning to tell Mrs. Edwards about the problems Glenn's been having?"

"Do you think I should?"

"You really want my opinion?"

She turned to look at him. "Yes, I do," she said, and was surprised to find that she did. She was used to discussing these matters with Sue, but she and Sue had been so busy discussing her relationship with Dillon, that she'd not discussed this issue. "So tell me."

"She needs to know that he's at an emotional time in his life, but I don't think she needs to know that he's had a discipline problem. It may color her expectations for him. And we don't want him to start out with any disadvantages."

Monique considered his words. "I think you're right. I was actually thinking the same thing. Besides, he's adjusting so well."

"We'll continue to keep an eye on him, though. We may not be out of the woods yet."

She placed her hand atop his resting on the steering wheel. "Thanks, Dillon," she said. "It feels good—and right—discussing this with you. I'd forgotten what it felt like to share this responsibility."

Dillon cleared his throat, and she wondered if he was fighting tears. "No problem," he said. "No problem at all."

Dillon was still feeling the residual good feelings of his morning talk with Monique and their subsequent meeting with Mrs. Edwards when he reached his parents' house later that afternoon.

Glenn and Calvin met him at the door with cheers and a list of requests. "Can I spend the night with Glenn, Daddy?" Calvin asked. "Please, Daddy?"

"Yeah, please, Dillon. Let him spend the night at my house."

Dillon couldn't have been more surprised or more happy about the request. He figured the relationship with the boys was now sealed. He rubbed a hand across each boy's head. "If it's all right with Monique, it's all right with me."

"Yay," both yelled.

"Hey," Dillon's mother said, coming to the front door to join them. She was dressed in an apron, which told him she was preparing dinner. "What's all the noise about?" she asked the boys.

"Daddy said I could spend the night with Glenn and Moni."

"Dillon said Calvin could spend the night at my house, Grandma."

"I told you he would." Mrs. Bell smiled at her grandsons. "Grandpa told me to tell you he had a surprise for you two."

The boys cheered again then headed for the back of the house and Grandpa.

Dillon shook his head. "Are you sure you're up for taking care of them every day, Ma? They're a handful."

"Nonsense," she said. "I love having them here and you know it."

He followed her when she turned and went back to the kitchen. "I didn't say you didn't like it, I just said they were a handful."

After looking out the window at his father and the boys in the backyard, Dillon pulled out a chair from the dinette table and sat down. His mother joined him after she checked the oven.

"Smells good," he said.

She grinned. "Yes, Dillon, you and Calvin are welcome to stay for dinner."

He grinned, too. "Thanks, Ma. I knew you'd ask."

"I know you did. I just hope Monique and Glenn will stay, too. There's more than enough food."

Dillon checked his watch. "I'm surprised she's not here already."

"She called and said she was running a little late. She should be here any minute."

He wondered what had kept her, but didn't bother asking his mother. If she'd known, she would have told him.

"She's done a good job with Glenn."

Dillon's attention was brought quickly back to his mother. A compliment for Monique was a definite departure for her. "She sure did. Monique's a great mother."

At that moment, the boys ran through the kitchen.

"Hey, hey," he called to them. "What's this running about? You two know better."

Still bouncing on his toes, Calvin said, "It's Moni."

"Yeah," Glenn added. "We saw Mom's car pull into the drive."

Dillon grinned. "Go on," he said. "But don't run," he added a bit too late. The boys were already back on the run.

"They were outside," Dillon said with a shake of his head. "So tell me why they ran inside so they could run outside again?" He laughed and so did his mother. "Please tell me, Ma, that I had more sense than that when I was their age."

"Sorry, but I can't even tell you that you had as much sense as they do. You and your brothers were something else."

Dillon would have denied her words, but the memory of him trying to ride his bike blindfolded presented itself. He shuddered to think of Calvin or Glenn doing something so stupid.

"Slow down, boys," he heard Monique say. There was a lilt in her voice that said she was enjoying herself.

Dillon watched as the boys, each holding one of her hands, practically dragged Monique into the kitchen. Her purse had fallen off her shoulder and hung loose at her elbow. Glenn was dragging her briefcase in his free hand. She looked adorable. And sexy as hell. He couldn't believe that he hadn't noticed earlier how her dress hung to her curves. Tight enough to be enticing, yet loose enough to be professional.

"Tell her, Dillon," Glenn said, breathless with excitement. "Tell her you said Calvin could spend the night with us."

Dillon looked up into Monique's smiling eyes. "If it's all right with you."

"Tell him it's all right, Mom, tell him."

"All right, Glenn," Monique said. "And you too, Calvin. You guys need to give me a minute to catch my breath."

"But it's all right, isn't it, Moni?" Calvin couldn't resist asking again.

Dillon watched as she managed to loosen her arms

from the boys' clutches. "Now," she said, pushing her bag back up her arm and stooping down. "Who's going to be the first to give me my afternoon hug?"

Calvin jumped in first while Glenn hung back. Clearly he thought hugging was more appropriate for his younger brother. Dillon's chest tightened as he watched Monique close her eyes and enclose his son in her warm embrace. When she finally let him go and opened her eyes, he saw pure joy in them.

"That was so good, Calvin," she said. "You'll have to give me one of those every day. All right?"

Calvin nodded and gave a shy smile.

"Who's next?" Monique said, looking at Glenn with a sly smile on her face. From the look the boy gave her, Dillon concluded that his son knew he was being blackmailed. Even so, he moved into his mother's arms for a brief embrace.

When he pulled away, Monique tweaked his nose. "Not bad, buster," she said lovingly. Glenn grinned in spite of himself.

"So, is it all right if Calvin spends the night with us?"

Monique stood and brushed a hand over each boy's head. "Sure, I think it's a great idea for Calvin to spend the night with us."

Dillon looked from his smiling and happy sons to the flushed and sexy Monique and felt a bit jealous that his sons would spend the night with her and he wouldn't.

Monique had been surprised—but very happy—when Glenn had asked if Calvin could spend the night with them in their new house. The brothers were becoming friends, and she couldn't ask for more. Fortunately, Dillon felt the same and allowed Calvin to stay over. Naturally, he came over and stayed until both boys were tucked in bed. Afterward, he and Monique sat in her new family room.

"I like the house," Dillon said. "You've made it homey in no time at all."

"Thank you," she said, nervous and hating herself for it. They were just talking. Nothing more. "It's a good house." She knew the two-story colonial was too big for her and Glenn, but she'd liked the yard and the house's proximity to Glenn's school and the park. She'd filled it with the furnishings from their old house so the place did have the family stamp on it.

They were silent for a while as the tension between them filled the room. Dillon cleared his throat, then spoke. "I'm glad you took Ma up on her offer," he said.

"I think it was a perfect solution," she replied. "But I hope your mother doesn't live to regret it." Mrs. Bell had suggested that she drop Glenn off at her house every morning until school started. She'd also volunteered to pick Glenn up after school and keep him until Monique got in from work each day after the school year began.

"Ma loves having both boys around. You couldn't have made her happier."

Monique felt she'd made a breakthrough with Katherine Bell at the picnic, and she looked forward to the day the two of them became real friends. She knew the woman's overtures at this point were because of her grandson. "Well, it made Glenn happy, too. And it works out perfectly for me. I don't have to worry about child care. I know he's with someone who cares about him as much as I do."

"That's important to you, isn't it?"

"Of course, it is," she said, thinking his question odd. "That's the biggest problem for working mothers. Back in Charleston, Sue took care of him for me. Now, your mother does."

"Have you spoken to Sue since you've been back?"

She nodded. "We talk frequently. She still hasn't agreed to move here, but I'm not giving up yet. I hate to think of her there all alone."

Dillon didn't respond. He just stared at her and Monique felt as though she stood in the middle of a blazing fire, the heat between them was so hot. "So, how's school?" she asked, then immediately felt stupid. It had to be obvious that she was fishing for a topic of discussion.

He raised a brow at her question. He knew what she was trying to do. And he also knew he should get up and go home, but he liked being in her presence. He'd gotten used to talking with her, being with her. That was not good, he knew, but that was the way it was. "I should be asking you. How was your first day?"

While she launched into a description of her day, he briefly wondered what life would be like if they didn't have separate homes. If he and Monique shared a bedroom down the hall from their boys. If they were the real family that it appeared they were.

But he had no right to those thoughts. His future held no room for Monique other than as Glenn's mother. Sure, in that role she would be a large factor in his life, but she wouldn't have the emotional hold over him that she'd had in the past. A hold that twice now had meant pain for him.

No, Monique was a woman to want from afar. And want her he did. Every day and almost all the time. But he was handling it. Day by day. Moment by moment.

As he looked at her now, dressed casually in jeans and a T-shirt, looking as fresh as a teenager and all animated as she talked about her new job, his resolve seemed to crumble. Being the adult he was, he had the perfect remedy for his predicament. He rubbed his hands down his jean-clad legs. "I guess I'd better go," he said, standing up.

"Oh, all right," she said, and he would have sworn that he heard disappointment in her voice. She stood up and led him to the door.

"I'll pick the boys up in the morning and take them to Ma's," he said after she'd opened the door for him.

"That's not necessary. I can take them."

"I know it's not necessary, but I like to have some time with them before I start the day. I guess I've gotten used to it since Calvin started staying at Ma's with Glenn every day."

"Well, if you're sure," she said.

"I'm sure. How about seven-thirty?"

"Seven-thirty's fine."

He stuffed his hands in his pockets. "I'll see you in the morning, then."

"Okay," she said.

He nodded, then turned and made his way down the walk. A part of Monique wanted to call out to him, to tell him that she didn't want him to go. But she knew such a move would be a disaster. So she waited until he'd started his truck and pulled out of her driveway. Then she closed the door and made her way to her lonely bedroom. She didn't have to wonder what she would dream about tonight. His face was already on her mind.

Chapter Twelve

Glenn was in bed, the house was quiet and Monique sat in the kitchen sipping her usual late-night cup of coffee. This had become her time of the day. A time to reflect on the day's happenings and make plans for tomorrow. She'd been in Elberton about six weeks now and Glenn had been in school about a month. In that time, she, Dillon and the boys had fallen into a routine that worked for all of them. Mrs. Bell picked the boys up from school each day, and they stayed at her house until Dillon and Monique came to pick them up. Most nights, she and Dillon would spend a few moments talking while the boys got their things together. On other nights, they'd spend the evening having dinner with the Bells.

Monique and Glenn had even been invited to share in the Sunday Bell family dinner, which ended with Mr. Bell taking the boys for a walk around the block.

And Calvin and Glenn spent the night together at her house, Dillon's or the elder Bells' at least one night a week, usually on the weekends. She couldn't have hoped for a better situation for Glenn...or for Calvin. She'd had her chance to show the little boy how much she cared for him, and she liked to think that it made a difference. She knew it made a difference to her.

She drank the last of her coffee, got up, rinsed out her cup and put it in the dishwasher. The quiet stillness of the night surrounded her, and she acknowledged that this time of the night, right after she'd finished her musing and before going to bed, was the lonely time of the day for her. She could no longer tell herself that she was alone—but not lonely—because she no longer believed it was true. Now that Glenn was doing better, she had more time to focus on her own needs. And the truth was, she was lonely for male companionship. Unfortunately, she was lonely for a particular male's companionship.

As she made her way up the stairs and went to run her bath, her thoughts turned to Dillon as they always did. She still fought the feelings she had for him, but she was slowly becoming accustomed to having them and not acting on them. She supposed he was, too. But the sexual attraction between them was there, alive and well, and, for now, under control. Surprisingly, school had become a place of reprieve for her. Though she and Dillon worked in the same building, they really didn't spend much time together now that she had established herself with the faculty. She saw him only occasionally, either in the hallways or at the weekly staff meetings.

She turned off her bathwater, then decided to give

Sue a call. Her sister-in-law picked up on the second ring.

"I was hoping you would call," Sue said with an unfamiliar breathlessness in her voice.

"Is anything wrong, Sue? You sound different."

"Oh, Monique," Sue said, and to Monique she sounded giddy. Yes, Sue sounded giddy. "I can't believe it."

Monique dropped down on the side of the bed. This behavior was so unusual for Sue. "What can't you believe?"

Sue drew a deep breath. "You'd better sit down."

"I'm sitting down," Monique said a bit anxiously.

"I'm getting married!"

"What?" Monique couldn't keep the surprise out of her voice.

"I'm getting married. Can you believe it?"

No, Monique couldn't believe it. She hadn't even known her sister-in-law was seeing anyone. Not that Sue wasn't an attractive woman—she was. Monique just hadn't known her to date. She wanted to be happy for the woman she loved, but warning signals went off in her head. "You sound happy," she said.

"Oh, Monique." This time Sue sounded like a teenager. "He's so wonderful. I never thought I'd meet anyone like him."

"Who is he, Sue?"

Sue giggled, actually giggled. "Wendell Freeman."

"Dr. Wendell Freeman?" Monique repeated. Wendell Freeman had been Charles's doctor and a lifelong family friend of the Morgans.

"Yes, Dr. Wendell Freeman. Isn't it wonderful, Monique?"

"Yes, Sue, that's really wonderful," she said, and meant it. Dr. Freeman had lost his wife a few years before Charles had passed away. Monique had come to know the doctor as a caring and honest man during the time he'd cared for Charles. "But I had no idea."

"I know you didn't, Monique. And I'm sorry for keeping it from you, but it only started recently."

Monique listened as Sue told her how her friendship with Dr. Freeman had grown into something more over the summer and had intensified in the time that Monique had been in Elberton. He'd asked Sue to marry him, and Sue had seen no reason to wait.

"I know this is fast, Monique, but I want you to be happy for me."

"I am happy for you, Sue. You of all people deserve to be happy. And you know that I couldn't think more highly of Dr. Freeman."

"Then why do you sound sad?"

Leave it to Sue to be so attuned to her feelings, Monique thought. "Because I'm selfish. I guess this means you won't be moving to Elberton with me and Glenn."

"No, dear," Sue said. "But you don't need me. You and Glenn are embarking on a new phase in your life. You don't need me around as a reminder of the past."

"Don't say that, Sue. Glenn and I will always need you. You're my family."

"Your family's gotten a lot larger now, Monique. You have Dillon and Calvin and all the Bells. And now my family has gotten larger, too. I have you and Calvin, and now Wendell and the Freemans. Don't be sad, sweetheart. Be happy for me. Be happy for both of us."

"Oh, Sue," Monique said, shaking off her sadness. "I'm happy for you. Now when's the wedding?"

"We've decided that we want something small, held here at the house since this is where we'll be living. Of course, you and Glenn and Calvin and Dillon have to be here."

"We wouldn't miss it for the world," Monique said, then launched into a discussion of the details of the event. Though she was happy for her sister-in-law, the news of Sue's upcoming marriage made her feel even lonelier.

When Dillon stopped by Monique's house that Friday with Calvin's clothes for his weekend with her and Glenn, he thought she appeared a bit distracted. "Is something wrong?" he asked.

"Oh, no," she said. "I'm fine."

He didn't believe her, but neither did he pursue the topic. "I wanted to talk to you about something," he said instead. "Do you have a few minutes?"

"Sure," she said. "Have a seat." She led him to the living room couch. "Would you like some coffee?"

"That would be nice." When she went to the kitchen, he followed her. "I wanted to ask you about the boys going with my parents when they visit Darnell in a couple of weeks."

"How long will they be gone?" she asked, pouring them both a cup of coffee. "You know Glenn has school."

He sat down at the kitchen counter. "I know. They'll only be gone for the weekend. Darnell wants the folks to come out to Dallas for a visit, and they want to take the boys with them. Of course, Darnell is eager to meet Glenn.''

She didn't answer and Dillon assumed she was reluctant to let Glenn go by himself. "If you don't feel comfortable with Glenn traveling with my parents, you can go with them."

She shook her head. "It's not that, Dillon. Sure, I'll miss Glenn, but I sort of like the idea of him spending time with his grandparents. It'll be good for him."

"Then what's the problem, Monique? I know something's wrong." He wanted to fix it, whatever it was. He didn't like seeing her upset.

She sat down. "I told you. There's nothing wrong. Wait a minute. What weekend is this trip?"

"The weekend after Halloween," he said. "Darnell wants the boys to attend this big Halloween celebration they're having at the hospital where he works. Is that going to be a problem?"

"I don't think so, but I need to check with Sue. She's getting married and, of course, she wants us there. You and Calvin are invited, too."

"That's great," Dillon said, genuinely pleased. He'd liked Sue a lot and thought she deserved happiness. "And tell her thanks for inviting me and Calvin. I'm honored."

"Well, she likes you a lot."

"I guess they haven't set a date."

She nodded. "Not yet. All Sue has said is soon."

"Well, let me know as soon as you find out. There's no rush. I'll let Ma know as soon as you tell me." He still wasn't convinced that Monique was okay, so he tried again. "Are you upset because Sue won't be moving to Elberton?"

She stared down at her coffee. "I know it's childish of me, Dillon, but Sue's been my family for a long time. I miss her. But I also want her to be happy."

Dillon realized that a lot had changed in Monique's life in the last few months. She'd left behind the home and the life she'd made for herself because of her love for her son. He admired her for loving Glenn enough to make that sacrifice, but he wondered if the life she lived now was enough for her. He'd often wondered about a woman like her being without a man, and he wondered about it again now. "Your life has changed a lot in the last few months, hasn't it, Monique?"

She looked up at him before staring down at her coffee cup. "I guess you could say that."

"Has it been worth it?" he asked.

"You really have to ask?"

He nodded. He thought he knew the answer but he wanted to hear her answer.

"When I look at Glenn and Calvin, I know I did the right thing. Glenn needed you and your family, Dillon. I'm convinced of that."

"But what about you, Monique?" he asked. "What do you need?"

She shrugged as if the answer to his question was inconsequential. "I just need for Glenn to be happy. That's all I need."

"You sound sure of that."

"I am."

"So, there's been no one special in your life since your husband died?" He remembered her telling him so once when they'd been visiting with Glenn at Sue's house. He reopened the topic now for other reasons.

"Just Glenn."

"And that's enough?"

She looked at him with wide, hungry eyes, and he wanted to wrap her in his arms, but her next words stopped him.

"I haven't seen you with anyone special, and you've said there's been no one since your wife. Were you lying?"

It was Dillon's turn to stare at his coffee cup. "No," he said.

"Then I guess we're in the same boat."

"What boat is that?"

"The boys, Dillon," she said. "You said before that your life was full with Calvin, and now I'd guess it's even fuller with both boys."

He looked at her with questioning eyes. "Seems it would have worked that way, doesn't it?" He decided to end the charade and try honesty. "Lately, I'm not too sure about how full my life is. I'm beginning to think that I need more than the boys."

She sucked in her breath, then picked up her cup. "Are you finished?" she asked.

He wasn't, but he nodded his head and she picked up his cup, too. He knew it was time for him to go home.

Luckily for Monique, Sue and Wendell planned their wedding for the weekend before the Bells' trip to visit Darnell. She flew up the day before the wedding to spend some time with Sue. Dillon and the boys flew up and joined them the morning of the wedding. She tried not to be disappointed that Glenn had preferred to wait and come with Dillon and Calvin rather than come early with her, but she hadn't really succeeded.

While she'd been very happy for Sue and Wendell—it was obvious how much they loved each other—she spent a great deal of time at the wedding feeling sorry for herself. It seemed everyone was getting on with their lives but her. She felt as though she was losing Glenn, and now she was losing Sue.

She went through the week after the wedding with a face of happiness, but inside she still felt sorry for herself. And she was getting tired of her own self-pity. She had a good life. Glenn and Calvin were happy and thriving; her job at the school was challenging and interesting; and her relationship with the Bells was good. She needed to pull herself out of this funk she was in and get on with the process of living her life. When she packed Glenn off with Calvin and his grandparents, she told herself she had until they got back to get herself together.

Not wanting to face a night at home alone, she went out for dinner at the Dinner Plate. As luck would have it, the first person she saw after she arrived was Dillon.

"Hi," he said. "I guess we're in the same boat. You missing them already?"

She accepted that excuse. "And I bet they haven't thought about us since they left."

He laughed. "I don't think I'll take that bet."

She smiled, too, because she couldn't think of anything to say.

"Hi, Mr. Bell, Mrs. Morgan."

Dillon and Monique greeted the young waitress, who was also a student at the high school.

"Two?" she asked.

Dillon queried Monique with his eyes. "I'm game if you are."

"Fine."

He turned back to the waitress. "Two."

When the waitress turned, he placed his hand on the small of Monique's back and followed the teenager to a booth near the salad bar. Monique told herself to ignore the warmth his touch caused to flow through her body.

"I think this is our table," he said. He must have seen the question in her eyes because he clarified his statement. "You were sitting here that first night Calvin and I joined you. You don't remember?"

Now she remembered, but she could think only of the tingling warmth that remained even though he was no longer touching her. "Oh, yes, I remember."

The waitress came back with water and menus, then told Monique and Dillon to help themselves to the salad bar.

"Are you going to order anything else?" Dillon asked as he studied the menu. "I think I'll try the prime rib tonight."

"Not me," she said. "I'm not that hungry."

He sensed something was wrong with Monique. In fact, he'd sensed it for a while now. Sure, she tried to cover it up, but he knew something was wrong. And he wished he could do something to help her. "The wedding got you down?" he asked, though from her obvious joy with Sue's happiness he didn't think her problem was with the wedding.

She shrugged her slight shoulders. "Not really. I'm just feeling kind of restless."

"Ahh... I think I know that feeling. Elberton is a small town. Maybe you need to expand your horizons a bit."

"And do what?" she asked.

He had a great idea, but he was hesitant to present it to her. After studying the sadness in her eyes for a few seconds, he decided to go for it. "When's the last time you've been dancing? Heard some good music?"

Monique couldn't remember the last time, and she told him so.

He pulled out his wallet and plopped a ten-dollar bill on the table. "That should keep the waitress from getting angry with us." He stood up and extended his hand to her.

"What are you doing?" she asked.

He didn't want to think about what he was doing. He just wanted to erase the sadness from her eyes. "How about some dancing and good music? Maybe even some tasty food thrown in for good measure?"

"I don't think—"

"Then don't think." He tried to shake off the hurt her reluctance caused. "We'll just have a little grown-up fun. I promise to get you home at a decent hour."

She stared at his hand, then let her gaze travel back to his face. A slow smile spread across her face as she placed her hand in his. "Do I need to change?" she asked.

He gave a full-length appraisal of her tan slacks and white silk blouse. She was perfect. He grinned at her. "Not a thing," he said. "Ready?"

Monique refused to think about what she was doing as Dillon wrapped his fingers around hers. She allowed him to escort her from her seat and out of the restaurant to her car. He suggested that she drive home and he'd follow. From there they would take his truck. She agreed. On the drive to her house, she considered changing her mind and not going with him. Then she told herself she was being silly, they were only going dancing.

Dillon tried to ignore the excitement he felt as he followed Monique. *You're only taking her out because she's sad,* he reminded himself. *There's nothing more to it.*

When she pulled into her drive, he hopped out of his truck and rushed to help her out of the car. Nothing wrong with that, he told himself. He was just being courteous. He almost believed himself until his hand brushed hers and she looked up into his eyes. Then he knew he was in trouble.

Chapter Thirteen

Monique knew she would like the Carlton Club as soon as she walked through its pink doors. She scanned the casually but well-dressed crowd and quickly concluded that most of the patrons ranged in age from late twenties to late thirties. A handsome waiter clad in gray slacks and a pink golf shirt greeted them and led them to a table in a corner near the dance floor.

"You didn't tell me they had a live band," she said.

"I told you we were going dancing. You should have known that I only go first-class."

She smiled. Dillon was flirting with her and she liked it. "Do you come here often?"

"Only when I have a pretty lady I'm trying to impress."

"And just how often is that?" she asked, determined to give as good as she got.

"Hmm, I don't think I should answer that one."

"Does that mean it's been a lot?"

He leaned forward slightly and she had the unnerving urge to kiss him. "That's not what it means at all," he whispered.

His words were a caress and she knew he was telling the truth. He hadn't brought anyone here in a long time. Any flip flirtatious comeback left her mind. Thankfully, the band chose that moment to start up again. Dillon held his hand out to her for the second time tonight. "You ready to give it a whirl?"

She graciously took his hand and slid into his arms. When she did, every bit of the restlessness she'd experienced fled, and she immediately felt as if she'd come home. This was what she'd been missing, what she'd been wanting. The strong masculine smell of his cologne filled her nostrils and she had to rest her body against his to keep from swooning.

Stop behaving like a besotted teenager, she chided herself, but the chastisement did no good. As she rested her head against his broad chest, she had to force herself not to burrow closer to him, to try and lose herself in him.

Somewhere in the recesses of her mind she realized they were moving a lot slower than the rest of the people on the dance floor and a lot slower than the music dictated, but it didn't matter. She felt dizzy just swaying with him on the floor. And now that she was in his arms, she didn't want to leave them.

She wondered if Dillon felt as whole as she did. The thump, thump of his heart matched hers and made her think that maybe he did. A sure way to know would be to look up into his eyes, but she rejected that option. She didn't trust herself to see her need reflected in his eyes. She was strong, but she wasn't that strong.

Dillon tightened his hold on Monique, though he knew he really should be releasing her so that they could dance like everyone else. But he didn't seem to be able to make his arms do what his mind dictated. Without fighting very much, he gave up and gave in. He admitted that he'd wanted the freedom to hold her ever since their first visit to Charleston. Monique was in his blood, and no amount of denial was going to make her go away.

The music stopped too soon for him, and he was forced to release her. He tilted her face up to his and was rocked by the need that he saw in her eyes. He licked his lips and fought the urge to kiss her. And how he wanted to kiss her.

She watched him and licked her lips, too. Aw, hell, he thought to himself, and lowered his head to hers, right there in the middle of the dance floor.

The first touch of his lips against hers ignited a long-simmering passion. He crushed her to him and increased the pressure. When she opened her mouth in sweet response, he wanted to shout his pleasure. Though he could have continued kissing her in that exact spot for the rest of the night, a voice in his head told him they should stop. He reluctantly lifted his head and looked down into her face, unsure what he would see reflected there despite her impassioned response. He was gratified to see pleasure in her features and a smile on her lips. He brought their still-entwined hands to his lips and kissed them. Then he led them back to their table.

Somehow they were able to order and eat a small meal, though he couldn't for the life of him remember what it was or how it had tasted. He'd spent the entire meal watching her eat and imagining how it would feel to have her lips all over his body. And his all over hers.

"You've got to stop looking at me like that," she finally said.

He grunted, unable to stop looking at her. He was a goner and there was no turning back. At least not tonight. He hoped she knew that. "Or what?" he challenged.

She opened her mouth to speak, but quickly closed it.

"Aw, hell." He threw some bills on the table and extended his hand to her for the third time. "Are you ready?"

As Monique stared at his outstretched hand, she realized his question was more than an inquiry as to whether she was ready to go home. No, Dillon was asking much more. If she thought about it, she would tell him she wasn't ready. She didn't think. She lifted her gaze to his and said, "I'm ready."

She sat close to Dillon on the drive back to Elberton. His arm rested across her shoulders and his fingers rubbed against her neck. His touch kept her from thinking about the mistake she was surely making. Neither spoke, seeming to know that conversation would spoil the mood. They were content to touch and just be.

When Dillon reached town, he asked, "My house?"

"Fine," she said, understanding that his car parked

in her drive all night was bound to cause gossip and speculation. She appreciated his thoughtfulness.

A few minutes later, he pulled his truck into his drive and shut off the engine. Before she could move out of his embrace, he pulled her closer for another soul-stirring kiss. This one was longer and more demanding than the one they'd shared at the club. She knew it was a preview of coming attractions.

He pulled back and looked down into her eyes. She saw the question there and knew that he was giving her one last chance to change her mind. She pressed her hand against his cheek and led him in a kiss that gave him her answer.

A low moan came from deep in his throat as he accepted what she so freely gave. This time when he pulled away, he opened his door with one hand and pulled her toward him with the other so that they both exited the truck from the driver's side.

He tucked her into the crook of his arm and guided her to his front door. After making quick work of opening the door, he released her hand and let her enter before him. She turned to watch him as he closed the door, then she walked back into his arms.

He crushed her to him. A happiness and a completeness he'd not felt in a long time washed over him. He didn't want to think what the feeling meant, so he directed all his energy, all his thoughts into her and into the kiss they shared.

This time she ended the kiss, pulling away from him and refusing to meet his eyes. Wondering what she was thinking, he tilted her head up. His heart shattered at the tears he saw in her eyes.

"What is it, sweetheart?" he murmured, kissing

each of her eyelids as if the touch of his lips could stop her tears.

"Oh, Dillon" was all she could say. And it was enough. He crushed her to him again. Her arms wound around his neck and she pressed her body full length against him. But it wasn't enough. Without breaking the kiss, he lifted her in his arms and strode down the hall to his bedroom. He kicked open the door with his foot and quickly made his way to the bed.

He eased her down and covered her with his own body. This was what he'd wanted for the last ten years. To hold her in his arms again. To join his body with hers. To be whole in her arms. He realized then that he hadn't been whole since the last time they'd been one. The jarring thought made him break the kiss and pull away from her.

The question and insecurity he saw in her eyes brought him back to her. She needed him and he needed her. They had to have this time together. They could figure out later what it all meant.

Monique felt a freedom she'd only felt in Dillon's arms. There was no doubt in her mind that here was where she belonged. She'd only been partially alive without him. She'd been alive, but she hadn't lived. Not until now.

Needing to feel his skin beneath her fingers, she worked her hand down his chest and tried to pull his shirt out of the waistband of his slacks. She groaned her frustration when she was unable to accomplish her goal. Tearing her lips from his, she murmured, "Too many clothes."

His gruff, passion-filled chuckle sent shimmers of pleasure through her veins. "I agree with you on that one, darling." He nipped at her lips while she tried again, this time successfully, to get his shirt off. Impatiently she pressed her hands flat against his chest before beginning an exploration of his upper body.

She touched him as if he were precious to her, and his heart almost popped out of his chest. Thinking she needed to get a little of what she was giving, he quickly undid her blouse, slipped it off her shoulders and threw it on the floor. He then pressed his lips against one cup of the thin lace bra that covered her breasts. Not satisfied, he made short order of removing the bra and sucking one firm nipple into his mouth.

Monique squirmed against him and he thought he was going to lose it. He had wanted to take it slow, but he now knew that was impossible. She was as eager and as ready as he was. There was no way for them to take this slow.

In a flurry of hands, kisses, zippers and groans of pleasure, they managed to undress each other. While he wanted to immediately sheath himself inside her, he was forced to give honor and homage to her beauty and to the passion that flowed between them. He kissed her again, while his hands became familiar with the changes in her body. It had been a long time, he thought. Much too long.

Monique accepted the pleasure that Dillon gave her and tried with all her might to return the same. She wanted him to know how much he meant to her, not just physically, but in her heart. She wanted him to know that she needed him emotionally as much as she needed him physically. And she wanted him to know that she needed him *now*.

"Dillon." His name was a moan on her lips, and

she realized she wouldn't be able to tell him what she wanted. She'd have to show him. In a display of feminine wantonness, she lifted her legs and rested them across his hips.

His answering groan told her that he had gotten her message. He lifted his head and his lower body at the same time. And she braced her hands on his arms as he positioned himself between her legs. She thought to tell him that it had been a long time, but she was not quick enough. In one smooth thrust, he was inside her.

Dillon couldn't believe how warm and tight she was. At that moment, he would have given everything he owned to stay inside her. This was life. He and Monique. One body. One heart.

She lifted her hips toward him in an age-old motion, and he joined her in her quest for release. He wanted this for her as much as—if not more than— he wanted it for himself, and he was determined to hold out until she got what she wanted.

He didn't have to wait long. He felt the tremor in her body, then saw the passion flare in her eyes right before her scream of pleasure told him she'd reached her goal. He reached his seconds later.

When Monique came back down to earth, Dillon was collapsed across her, his body deadweight. He was heavy, but it was a good heavy. She cherished the feel of him against her and kissed his shoulder to tell him so.

"Am I too heavy?" he asked.

She shook her head, then realized he couldn't see her. "You're perfect," she said and meant it. He *was* perfect. He was the perfect father and the perfect lover.

He raised up and looked down into her eyes. "I bet you say that to all your lovers."

She lowered her eyes and felt immediately shy before him.

He kissed her eyelids. "Please don't do that. I'm sorry. I was only teasing."

She still didn't look at him.

"Please, sweetheart. Don't leave me." He kissed her lips lightly. "Don't leave me."

She didn't fight his kiss, and when he pulled away she did look at him. He was so dear to her. So dear that he could break her heart if she allowed him.

"No regrets?" he asked.

She shook her head.

He nipped at her lips again. "Good."

She would have liked to hear more than "Good," but she knew the words wouldn't be worth much if she had to ask for them. "I think I'd better get dressed," she said, feeling the moment was over. What they'd shared had been beautiful from her perspective, but now the reality of their situation faced her. Nothing had changed between them.

"Why?" he asked, rolling off her and pulling her snugly into his arms. "I don't want you to go."

She wanted to ask him why, but settled for relaxing against him. "I'm going to have to go home sometime," she said.

He stroked his fingers across her taut nipples while he pressed light kisses across her face. "Why?"

For the life of her she couldn't think of an answer. She didn't want to. Following his lead, she took up the exploration of his body she'd begun earlier. His skin was warm and smooth and she wanted to touch every inch of it.

Feeling a boldness that was new to her, she rolled over until she sat across his lap as he lay on the bed. She watched his eyes widen and his lips open as she massaged his chest, taking special care to tweak his nipples much as he'd done to hers.

His groan of pleasure encouraged her, and she became bolder in her touch. She leaned down and suckled first one nipple and then the other, marveling at their tautness and at the pleasure her lips seemed to give him.

She moved from his chest up to his neck and to his mouth. She started the kiss, but he took over and soon she was again flat on her back with him poised above her like a bronze god. Her bronze god.

Dillon didn't think he could let her go. Not now. Not tonight. Maybe not even tomorrow. He hadn't liked the panic he felt when she'd said she wanted to get dressed. He couldn't let her leave him now. They had too much time to make up for. There was no way that one night would be enough for him. Had they not gone this far, maybe he could have continued to deny himself. But having tasted her again, he knew there was no way he could do without her.

He stared into her eyes, loving the play of emotions that danced in them. He saw a passion and a hint of fear that he knew were mirrored in his own eyes. He knew there were questions between them. But whether they needed to make love wasn't one of them. No, the lovemaking they shared now was essential for both of them. He was sure of it.

He eased himself into her again, not able to wait any longer. Her eyes widened and the pressure of her hands on his arms increased as he sought refuge within her. He thought again about her tightness, her wetness and her warmth. She was perfect. And for now, she was his.

When he was fully seated within her, he stopped moving. He just stared into her eyes and let his heart speak for him. He wanted her to know that he didn't take what they shared lightly. It was only when he thought she understood that he began to move again, starting with long, slow strokes that teased both of them.

She matched his motion and they soon fell into a sweet rhythm that he knew would end in a crashing refrain. Her soft hands caressed his chest and her sweet kisses followed them, imprinting her touch all over his body. His pace increased with the boldness of his strokes, and soon they were near the precipice again. He deliberately slowed his pace to give her more time.

Monique knew Dillon wanted to make this time slower and sweeter, but she didn't want slow and sweet. She wanted hot and fast. "Now," she murmured, lifting her hips against him. "Now."

Dillon didn't need much coaxing. He immediately picked up the pace and gave her what she wanted.

Chapter Fourteen

Monique awoke to the warmth of Dillon's breath on her bare breast and his strong arm wrapped around her waist. She felt a moment of sheer bliss, a rightness between herself and the world around her, which she knew was because of him and what they'd shared. Magical moments. Moments that erased all time and all pain. Moments of giving and receiving.

The first time she and Dillon had made love, they'd been young, inexperienced and very much in love. Tonight she'd felt much the same. Dillon made her feel alive and much younger than her twenty-eight years. She was a kid again, with all the hopes that happy, well-adjusted kids had. There was something about him, and her with him, that made her think dreams could come true.

She brushed her hand lightly across his head and placed a soft kiss against his brow. In his sleep, he looked as innocent as Glenn or Calvin. And he also looked content and happy. It pleasured her to know that she was responsible for that contentment and happiness. Or, at least, part of it. She kissed his brow again, enjoying the opportunity to give him yet more of herself. She'd given him her body and her soul earlier, and now she was giving him her heart.

He doesn't want your heart, a harsh voice much like her aunt's said inside her head. All he wanted was your body, and you've already given that to him.

She squeezed her eyes shut and wanted to press her hands to her ears to keep the sounds away from the paradise she'd found. She didn't want reality to invade. Not yet. She needed more time.

She traced a finger down Dillon's jaw and thought of the many caresses and kisses they'd shared in the past few hours. More than she could count. Yet not enough. Not nearly enough. At least not for her. She wasn't so sure about him.

She dropped her hand to her side and no longer touched him. How she wished she could slip from this bed and his presence without having to face him. Without having to see the regret that she feared would be in his eyes. She much preferred to end the evening with the memory of the heated passion that had glazed his eyes each time he'd entered her, or the caring contentment she saw there each time he carried her over the edge. Those were the expressions she wanted to carry in her heart. All would have been right with the world if she could have taken what they'd shared tonight, bottled it and wore it as her own personal scent. A beautiful memory of a wondrous evening of love.

She looked down at him sleeping so peacefully and

fought the urge to close her eyes and snuggle against him. No, now wasn't the time to snuggle, she told herself. Now was the time to take action. To prepare herself for Dillon's response to what they'd shared.

Gently she tried to ease her body away from his. She managed to free her breast from contact with his head, but he clamped his arm tighter around her waist to keep her from moving away from him. She glanced back at him, thinking he'd awakened, only to find him still sleeping. The overhead light, still on since neither of them had had the energy to get up and turn it off before drifting off to sleep around two, illuminated the contented features of the masculine face that was so dear to her.

Again she considered sliding back against him. But she knew that was impractical. She couldn't spend the night with Dillon. Elberton was too small a town with too much of a penchant for gossip for her to even consider the idea. No, she had to get home tonight. She couldn't risk someone seeing Dillon drive her home in the morning.

She pushed at his arms to no avail. The more she pushed, the tighter he seemed to hold on. She glanced at his face again. This time she saw a twitch in his lips.

"Dillon, are you awake?" she asked.

He smiled and she went all soft inside. She fortified her resolve not to slide down next to him and let him take advantage of her softness.

"Where are you trying to go?" he asked. His fingers massaged the smooth skin of her waist and she almost forgot his question.

"I have to go home," she said, fighting the urge to return his caress. "It's late."

"Stay," he whispered. "Please stay."

His words rocked her as his earlier caresses had. But she couldn't stay. "I can't spend the night here," she said. "People will talk. Think about the boys."

His hands stopped their caress and he opened his eyes. "Think about us."

That was the problem. She could barely think of anything or anyone but them. She pushed again at his arms and this time he relaxed his hold and allowed her to get up. His masculine perusal of her naked body when she slid out of the bed put her at a distinct disadvantage. He wanted her again, and his eyes told her so. She was sure hers told him the same thing.

She shook her head to break the spell he'd cast over her and turned around to look for her clothes. His warm body pressed behind her before she could pick up her blue satin panties from the floor.

"Stay," he whispered again, then proceeded to place teasing kisses along her neck and shoulders.

God help her, she was weakening. "I can't, Dillon, and you know it." His kisses continued and she had to fight not to give in to them. "What will people think when they see you taking me home in the morning? By tomorrow afternoon, everybody in Elberton will know we spent the night together."

Dillon knew he needed to take Monique home. And not only for the reason she'd stated. Sure, they needed to be careful of the gossips because of the boys. But he also knew he needed to take her home before she burrowed herself any deeper under his skin. He didn't even want to think about his heart.

But he didn't seem to be able to let her go. He turned her around and kissed her full on the lips, causing the protest he saw forming there to die before it was fully formed. She tasted so good to him, so sweet. Apples, he thought. Red, luscious apples.

And she gave so generously. Even now, when he knew she was serious about leaving for the night, she gave. Her slim arms slid up his chest and around his neck as she pressed her naked body close to him. His body rose in response to her closeness, and he was sure she could feel how much he wanted her.

A voice inside his head told him again that he was getting in too deep, that he needed to be careful. *Fool me once* the thought began, but he lost it when she slipped her tongue in his open mouth and set about raising his body temperature a good twenty degrees.

She pulled away first, sighing then resting her head against his chest. "I still have to go home," she said.

He groaned at the need he felt. The need he knew would go unmet tonight. "I know," he said, then stepped back from her, not bothering to hide his arousal.

Her glance slid down then back up to his face before she turned and slipped on her panties. He sat back on the bed and watched her dress, thinking how odd for him to be so aroused at her putting *on* her clothes. Then he realized he was jealous of her clothes. Jealous because they rested against her naked skin. Jealous because they were filled with her scent. Man, he *was* losing it.

She didn't turn to him until she was fully clothed. "You're not dressed," she accused.

The practical side of his nature knew he was about to commit a grave error, but that side didn't have a chance against the side that still needed Monique. He extended his hand to her. "Please," he said. "I need you."

Monique could have resisted most any other plea, but she couldn't resist his "I need you" and the accompanying lack of regret in his eyes. She placed her hand in his. "I need you, too, but we have to think about the boys."

He tugged on her hand and she tumbled down on his lap. "I am thinking about the boys," he said, laving his tongue against her ear.

"You don't act like it." She squirmed on his lap when one of his hands tugged at her blouse. "You have to take me home."

He managed to get her blouse out of the waistband of her trousers, then slid his hand underneath and touched the bare skin of her stomach. "Okay," he said. "I'll take you home."

"When?" she asked as she opened her mouth for his kiss.

When the kiss ended, they were both breathless. "When?" she asked again.

"Sunday," he answered then kissed her again. This time his hand worked at the buttons of her blouse. Once they were all undone, he slipped her blouse down her shoulders and onto the floor.

"Sunday?" she managed to choke out. His fingers were now working at the hooks on her bra while she waited eagerly for the feel of his hands on her bare breasts. "What will people say?"

He kissed her again. "They won't say anything because they won't know anything. Your car is parked at your house, so for all everybody knows you're home now."

"But tomorrow," she protested, then moaned when his fingers tweaked one of her nipples.

Dillon made quick work of getting her out of her

slacks and panties, so that she was again naked against him. "Don't worry about tomorrow," he said, pressing her back onto the bed. "You're not leaving this bed until Sunday when we go pick up the boys."

Any protests Monique had were smothered in his tender and not-so-tender caresses.

The soft lushness of Monique's body sprawled across his chest called to Dillon when he awoke from their last bout of lovemaking. Even in her sleep, she mesmerized him, entranced him, beckoned him. And he was unable and unwilling to ignore the pull.

He lowered his head to kiss her and a noise caught his attention. He looked down at the sleeping Monique before easing her gently away from his body. It only took him a few moments to realize the source of the noise. He quickly got up from the bed and tugged on the pants he'd so hastily discarded the night before. He was definitely going to have to get his key back from Donald.

Sure enough, when he got to the front of the house, Donald, still dressed in his police uniform, was scrounging through his refrigerator.

His brother pulled a pitcher out of the fridge and grabbed a glass from the cabinet. "You've got to start stowing some brewski, my brother," Donald said, pouring himself a glass of grape juice. "This stuff is for the birds."

Dillon strode to his brother, placed the juice back in the refrigerator and closed the door. Then he extended his open palm. "My key," he said, wiggling his fingers in request. "How many times have I told you to knock?"

Donald looked at his brother's open palm then at

his face. He turned and walked, glass of juice in hand, to the living room and plopped down on the couch. "It's been a heck of a night," he said, propping his feet on Dillon's coffee table.

Dillon chastised himself for being so hard on his brother. "What happened?" he asked, concerned. He'd not been particularly happy with Donald's chosen profession. His brother sometimes seemed too carefree for the life-threatening job of policeman. But Donald had shown himself to be a capable and responsible officer. Dillon didn't worry about him as much as he had when he'd first gotten on the force, but he still worried.

"Family dispute." Donald swigged his glass of juice. "Man, I hate those things."

Dillon nodded, understanding his brother's feelings. Having grown up in a secure and stable family, neither Bell brother could fully understand families in distress. "Who was it?" Dillon asked.

Donald placed his glass on the table and wiped both his hands down his face. At that moment, Dillon wished for the teasing, carefree brother who at most times drove him crazy. "The Graysons," he said. "Who else?"

The Grayson family was Elberton's current family in crisis. As vice principal, Dillon had had his share of interactions with the family. An alcoholic father, a scared wife and a teenage daughter meant trouble more days than not. "Was it bad?" Dillon asked.

"The girl ran away," Donald said. "She ran away." He looked at his brother. "A fifteen-year-old girl ran away from home, and her parents are fighting about whose fault it is. Tell me, where's the justice in that?"

Dillon placed a hand on his brother's shoulder and squeezed. He didn't have any answers for him. Life was hard for a lot of people. And unfair though it was, sometimes the people that it was hardest on were children. He'd hoped that the Grayson girl would somehow beat the odds. He regretfully accepted that the school system could only do so much for a child.

He glanced toward the door to the room in which Monique lay sleeping peacefully. Her life hadn't been the easiest. She and her aunt had never really gotten along. And as close as he and Monique had been, she'd never really talked about her problems. Sure, she'd made some vague comments about her aunt not really wanting her, but he hadn't had the experience then to understand fully what that had meant. To him, family were people you could count on no matter what. Sure, they disagreed—even argued—but when it was over, they stood together. Not so with Monique and her aunt, and not so with the Graysons.

And now the Graysons' teenage daughter had run away. He knew things must have been pretty bad for the teen to leave and try to face life alone rather than stay and work it out with her parents. He prayed she would be all right.

"She's just a kid, Dillon," Donald said. "She has no idea about the crazies out there."

Dillon felt his brother's pain and had the sudden, but strong urge to call his boys. To hear their voices and make sure they were okay.

Donald proceeded to stretch out on the couch. "You mind if I crash here for a few? I don't feel like driving home right now."

Dillon cast a quick glance at his bedroom door again. What could he say? "Why don't you crash in

Calvin's room?" he suggested casually. "The bed is much more comfortable."

Donald shook his head and pulled one of the sofa pillows behind his head. "This is fine. I'll just crash for a while then go home. You go back to bed. I'll let myself out."

After Donald was settled, Dillon strode back to his bedroom. Monique was awake and sitting up when he returned.

Her eyes were anxious. "Is something wrong?" she asked.

He locked the bedroom door and took quick strides to her, needing to hold her again. "It's Donald," he said, then proceeded to tell her the story Donald had told him.

"That's awful, Dillon."

"I know," he said. "She's much too young to be out on her own."

Monique wondered at the compassion in Dillon's voice. He seemed genuinely concerned for the young girl. She wondered why he couldn't see the similarities between her and the Grayson girl.

"Sometimes people have to make hard choices, Dillon," she said. "Sometimes the risk of being on one's own is better than the risk of staying."

He looked down into her eyes and she knew he knew she'd been talking about herself. He squeezed her to him. "God, I was so worried about you," he said, his voice full of pain. "I couldn't believe you had left on your own. I just knew something awful had happened. I've never been so scared in all my life."

She felt his pain and she hated that she'd inflicted it on him. "I'm sorry, Dillon." She knew her words were inadequate, but they were all she had. "I'm so sorry that you had to go through that."

He continued to hold her, but neither spoke. Though she was still in his arms, the tone of their time together had changed. The past had intruded upon them like a splash of cold water. She wondered if it would always be between them, or if they could somehow get past it. The fact that she was in his bed said that she hoped they could.

Her dreams and her demons were staring her in the face right now. The fact that Dillon still held her in his arms told her that the dream she'd long held of a life with him was possible. But she recognized that the demons that threatened to ruin any chance of that ever occurring hovered nearby. She tried to concentrate on the dream and ignore the demons. This time she would fight fate to the end to get what she wanted.

Hours later, Monique still lay in Dillon's arms. She knew he was wide-awake even as she was. Too much was going on between them for either of them to sleep. She wanted to know what he was thinking, but she didn't know how to start the painful discussion. She contented herself to rest in his arms.

A short while later, she heard movements in the outer room and concluded that Donald was leaving. The click of the front door confirmed it. She looked up at Dillon, intending to say something about Donald, but the barely contained passion in his eyes stopped all words.

"I need you," he said as he'd said earlier in their evening together. "I need you so much."

And then no words were necessary. He lowered his head to hers and took her mouth in a kiss that began with an acknowledgment of all that was uncertain between them. His tentativeness almost broke her heart. She pressed her hand against his chest and pushed him back on the bed. Her lips fought with his to control the kiss. His groan told her that he'd given in to her. In response, she proceeded to make love to his mouth while her hand paid homage to the contours of his perfect male body.

The kiss that had begun tentatively, now burned like brushfire between them. Dillon wrapped his hands in her hair and pressed her closer. Her body was flat against his from chest to thigh, and she loved the feel of him. Of her against him.

It was only natural that her body sought him and found him. When they merged in the way of lovers, the past was forgotten and they were one. If what they had now could only last, was Monique's final thought before he transported her to their own personal paradise.

Chapter Fifteen

Dillon stared down into Monique's contentedly sleeping face and decided to stop fighting. Her constant presence in his life made it impossible for him to ignore the potent attraction that flamed so brightly between them. And after making love with her, he knew any effort to fight that attraction would be futile.

Unable to resist the temptation that she presented, he leaned down and placed a light kiss against her sweet lips.

"Mmm," she murmured, those enticing lips turned in a smile. "I like that."

He sank down in the bed and pulled her closer in his embrace. "You stinker," he said, "I thought you were asleep."

She opened her eyes and they, too, were smiling. "I was."

He patted her bare rump. "If you had been asleep, that little kiss would not have awakened you."

Her eyes grew serious and dark. "It wasn't the kiss that woke me."

"What was it, then?"

She touched her palm to his cheek. "I felt you looking at me. That's what woke me."

He groaned, understanding the truth and the depth in her words. It was that connection that had always existed between them. It was still there, and both were powerless against it.

"What's happening between us, Dillon?" she asked.

He increased the pressure of his arms around her. "I'm not sure."

"You're not?" He heard the skepticism in her voice.

"I don't want to analyze it right now, Monique. I just want to go with it." She didn't say anything and he wondered where her thoughts were. "I want what's between us and with the boys to continue. That's all I know right now."

Monique knew a lot more about her feelings than Dillon knew about his. She knew that she was as in love with him now as she'd been as a teenager. She even wondered if she didn't love him more. She wasn't the same needy teenager she'd been then. She was a grown woman. A woman with options. A woman who knew her worth as a person and who knew that men—many men—found her attractive. Dillon was her heart, but he was no longer her lifeline.

She peered into his eyes and the passion she saw there made fresh the memory of their night of lovemaking. Dillon might not want to talk about his feelings, but she knew he definitely had them. A man couldn't make love to a woman the way he'd made love to her without some very strong affection for her. Maybe even a little love.

Monique also knew he wasn't the kind of man to take a woman to his bed carelessly. Had he been, there would have been a woman in his life when she'd returned to town. But unless the single women in Elberton were blind and crazy, he'd been alone by choice. Surely that she was in his bed meant something even if Dillon wasn't ready yet to voice it.

She smiled. "I'm hungry. You forced me to stay the night. Now aren't you going to feed me?"

He playfully swatted her rear again, this time allowing his touch to end in a caress. "Forced you?"

She rolled out of his embrace. "You don't play fair. You know that, don't you?"

His long arm reached out and brought her back to him. "I play to win. To hell with fair." He kissed her roughly across her mouth.

"Now, Dillon," she chided when she could breathe again. "What would the boys say if they heard you talk that way?"

"If you're thinking about the boys at a time like this, I must be doing something wrong."

He looked so hurt, Monique almost laughed. She placed her hand flat against his hard chest and followed with her mouth as she placed light kisses across his pecs. "You're not doing anything wrong," she said.

He groaned, then leaned back and dragged her across his body. Her breasts were pressed almost flat against his chest, and his mouth seemed to want to swallow hers. She loved it. She loved him.

"Dillon," she said between kisses.

"Hmm."

He caught her mouth in another long kiss, one that made her body tingle all over. "Dillon." His name was a moan this time.

"Tell me what you want," he ordered in a voice thick with need. "Tell me."

Monique fought hard to gather her wits, but it was difficult with his hands seeming to touch her all over her body at the same time and his mouth seeming to want to explore every crevice of hers. This man would consume her if she allowed him.

"Tell me what you want, Monique," he said again.

Though more than anything in the world, Monique wanted Dillon inside her again, she knew they couldn't spend the rest of the day in bed. Her mind fought with her heart and body over that conclusion and her mind won. "I want..."

"Tell me," he urged.

She accepted another kiss, then broke contact and propped her elbow on his chest. "I want bacon and eggs."

She did laugh at the expression that crossed his face then. But before she finished her laugh, he'd rolled her over and sank himself deep into her body. In the end, neither of them was laughing.

On Monday morning, Dillon leaned against Monique's open office door and watched her mouth expletives at her computer. It felt good standing in her space and knowing that she wanted him there as much as he wanted to be there. "I don't think that thing responds well to cursing."

She spun around in her chair and gave him a grim smile. "Well, nothing else is working. I thought I'd give it a try."

He pushed away from the door and walked toward her. "Want me to help?"

"Help yourself." She got up and pointed to her chair. "I don't think it likes me."

He cast a quick glance at Monique's door and seeing no one in the hallway, he planted a brief kiss across her lips. "You look adorable when you're frustrated." He smiled into her darkening eyes then took a seat, making a pretense of rolling up his sleeves. "Now let's see what a man can do."

She playfully slapped him across his shoulders. "You're the reason Calvin and Glenn are such young chauvinists. Now, get this thing to work and stop being so macho."

He looked up at her and wiggled his brows. "I thought you liked it when I got all macho." He sucked in his breath at the passion that flared in her eyes. "Don't look at me like that," he cautioned.

She lowered her lashes and leaned back against her desk, not saying anything. His eyes traveled from her soft leather red pumps up her smooth, firm calves to just above her knees where her skirt stopped. Sighing, he looked into her eyes. "If only—" he started, then shook his head. He wanted her. Real bad. But there was nothing he could do about it now. He turned back to the computer.

"It was working fine. Then it just locked up on me. Do you think you can fix it?"

"No problem." He hit the control-alt-delete sequence and rebooted the system.

Monique got up and leaned over his shoulder. "What are you doing?" she asked, her tone full of anxiety.

"I'm rebooting the system," he explained calmly. "That's a surefire way to end a lockup."

"I could have done that, Dillon." Her lips turned in a frown. "Now you've lost my file."

"Oh, ye of little faith," he said, shaking his head. "Now, would I lose your file?"

Her pert nose wrinkled in uncertainty. "You wouldn't do it on purpose, but—"

"But nothing," he said. "Now watch this." He executed the program she'd had open when he rebooted the system. "See." He pointed at the recovery file on the screen. "Is that your file?"

She leaned closer and her breasts brushed against his shoulder, causing his body to come to attention. She jumped away from him, obviously affected by their contact.

"Ah, let me see."

As she studied the screen, Dillon studied her. He remembered every curve of her body because he'd touched every curve, kissed every curve and loved every curve. The memory of the two days they'd spent together over the weekend would always be with him. The first time he'd held her, he'd been a boy. A boy in love, yet still a boy. But this past weekend, he'd been a man. And while he hadn't been in love—he no longer allowed himself that luxury—he'd felt deeply, even more deeply than he'd felt when he'd first loved her. There was something about Monique that would always bind him to her. It was his weakness, and he'd no longer fight it.

"So, is your file all there?" he asked, bringing his thoughts back to the present.

She turned back to him and gave him a smile that made his insides churn. "Yes, thank you, Dillon. You've saved my life."

"Well," he said. "I guess that means you owe me."

She lifted a questioning brow. "I'm afraid to ask what your price is."

"No need to be afraid. At least, not this time. I was just wondering if you and Glenn would have dinner with me and Calvin tonight. My house. I'm cooking."

Monique smiled. "I'm not sure. Calvin doesn't speak too highly of your culinary skills. Maybe you should offer to take us out to dinner instead."

He shook his head. "No way. My house. And I prepare the dinner." He didn't know why it was so important, but he wanted her and his son in his house tonight.

"What are you cooking?"

"Does it matter?"

Her gaze met his. "Not really," she said, and he was pleased that she didn't pretend coyness. "What time do you want us there?"

"Why don't I pick Glenn up at Ma's? That way you can go home, change clothes and relax a little before coming over."

She nodded. "Sounds good to me. I'll get over around six or so. Is that okay?"

"Fine," he said, walking to her door. He glanced in the hallway. Seeing no one, he closed and locked the door. In short strides, he was at her side. "I've got to touch you," he said, brushing a kiss down her cheek.

"But—" she murmured.

"No buts." He took her mouth in a kiss that left both of them wanting more. When he finally lifted his head, he brushed his thumb across her lips. "I had to do that."

She nodded understanding.

"I missed you last night," he whispered. "I don't know if I'll be able to sleep in that bed again without thinking about you. And wanting you."

"Dillon," she pleaded, her eyes bright with passion.

"Okay, I'll stop now, but only because we're at work. Tonight all bets will be off."

Her eyes widened. "The boys, Dillon."

He tapped her nose with his finger. "I'm not going to ravish you on the dining room table," he assured her.

She frowned. "Why, thanks. Now I feel a lot better."

He strode to her door and unlocked it. "Don't worry so much. The four of us will have fun tonight. I promise you."

It was exactly six o'clock when Monique pulled into Dillon's driveway. They were playing with some other boys in the neighborhood. This was the life she'd wanted for her son. He was happy here. And Calvin was happy with him.

The two boys left their friends and met her at the car, both talking at the same time. She gave each one an ear and tried to understand what they were talking about. She gathered it had something to do with Dillon's plans to take them camping.

"Camping?" she asked.

"Yeah, Mom," Glenn said. "It's gonna be great. We're going to sleep outside and cook on a fire and everything."

"You are, are you?" The boys' enthusiasm was evident by their bright eyes and fast-moving lips. "Are you inviting me to come along on this trip?"

Calvin looked at Glenn, who said, "Aw, Mom, you're a girl."

Somehow that response didn't surprise her. She shook her head, thinking she and Dillon were going to have to have a very long talk about the roles of boys and girls. "And what's that supposed to mean?"

The boys shrugged, then ran back to their friends. She shook her head again and headed for the front door. She knocked, but when no one answered, she opened the door and let herself in. As soon as she stepped across the threshold, the memory of the nights she'd spent here with Dillon filled her mind. A warm flutter started in her stomach and moved throughout her body. She felt good being here. Right, almost.

"Hey, I didn't hear you come in," Dillon said when she entered the kitchen. The sight of him in his jeans, sweatshirt and white apron tickled her. She'd bet more men than women wore aprons these days.

"I let myself in when you didn't answer," she said, taking a seat at the round dinette table. "It smells good. What is it?"

He flashed her a smile. "It does smell good, doesn't it? It's lasagna. My own special recipe."

"Not bad," she said, then paused for effect. "For a man."

He pressed a hand to his chest in mock offense. "You wound me. Why would you say something like that?"

She shook her head at his antics. "Dillon, we've got to do something about Glenn and Calvin. They're turning into little chauvinists. At first, I thought it was only natural that they wanted to spend time alone with you. After all, they're little boys and aren't yet interested in girls. But now I'm beginning to get worried. I don't want them to grow up thinking there are things women can't do."

Dillon pulled out a chair next to her and sat down. His face turned serious. "What happened?"

She placed her hand atop his to ease his worry, and he entwined their fingers. His strength and his warmth flowed to her, and she was comforted even as she sought to comfort him. "It's nothing really serious. At least not yet."

"But something happened to make you say what you did." He applied pressure to her hand. "What was it?"

"This camping trip you're taking them on. I asked if I could go and their response was that I was a girl."

Dillon smiled, then brought their entwined hands to his lips. He softly kissed each of her fingers. "Well, I know how to handle that," he said.

His lips on her hands caused the flutter in her stomach to expand. "Well, tell me, because I don't know how."

"It's simple," he said, tugging on her hand and pulling her closer to him. "You'll go camping with us."

Before she could speak, Dillon had pulled her onto his lap and captured her mouth with his. She felt the excitement in his body and in his kiss as she surrendered to his assault on her senses. She'd wanted this since he'd come to her office at school earlier in the day. When the kiss ended, she rested her head against his chest and enjoyed his closeness. She couldn't help but wish they could share a part of every day this way.

"When and where are we going on this camping trip?" she finally asked.

"The boys didn't tell you?"

She shook her head.

He chuckled. "*When* is the weekend before Thanksgiving. The *where* is nowhere. We're going to have our camp-out—complete with sleeping bags and a campfire—right here in the backyard."

"You're kidding. You can't have a campfire in your backyard."

His large hands caressed her breasts through her blouse. "Don't worry about it. I have friends in the police department."

"Are you sure?"

"Sure, I'm sure. Anyway, our campfire is going to be one of those hibachi grills. The boys will love it and it won't be dangerous at all, if that's what you're worried about."

"That's not it. I know you wouldn't do anything to harm the boys, Dillon."

He turned her face to his. "Then what is it?"

"I just didn't know we'd be *here*."

"Where would you suggest?"

She tried to twist out of his arms, but he held her

close. "I just thought we were going someplace else."

He kissed her lips again. "Tell me what's really wrong, Monique."

"What are people going to think if I'm spending the night here?"

"They're probably going to think you're spending the night here."

"You know what I mean."

He sighed. "Are you saying you don't want people to know we're seeing each other?"

"Is that what we're doing? Seeing each other?"

He nodded. "That's what I'd call it. What would you call it?"

She didn't answer. She didn't know what to call it. She knew what she felt when they were together, and she knew she wanted to build something with him. She guessed he wanted something similar, but he'd never said so. She realized now that she needed him to verbalize his intentions.

"Well, what would you call it?" he asked again.

"I guess we are seeing each other."

He pushed her off his lap and swatted her on her bottom. "Well, now that we've solved that dilemma, I can finish my meal. Why don't you set the table?"

"Is that my payment for dinner?"

His eyes met hers and they were dark and challenging. "Oh, no," he said. "You'll know when you're paying up and, believe me, you'll enjoy it."

She believed him.

Chapter Sixteen

Monique thought about Dillon as she packed up to leave her office on the Friday of the planned campout. He hadn't stuck his head in her office all day, and she'd missed seeing him. She contented herself with the knowledge that she would run into him at his mother's when she went to pick up Glenn. Though they hadn't made dinner plans, she'd decided to invite him and Calvin to join her and Glenn. She told herself the invitation was for the boys.

Shaking her head, she closed her briefcase. Why was she lying to herself? This invitation to dinner tonight was for her. She needed to see Dillon, to be with him. And she needed it often. They hadn't made love since the weekend the boys were away, and she felt she was going to explode if they didn't find some time to be alone. Tonight's dinner would be torture for both of them, she knew, but worse torture would be not spending any time at all with him today.

"Hi, beautiful," a smooth, masculine voice called from her doorway.

She didn't have to look up to know it belonged to Dillon. Her heart jumped into high gear and she wanted to hurl herself into his arms. "Hi, yourself, handsome," she said, settling for joining him in sexual repartee. She couldn't resist the temptation with a man who looked as sexy as he did in his plain, navy suit.

He pushed away from the door, closing and locking it behind him even though the students were gone for the day and few staff members were around. "How I've wanted to hold you all day," he said, taking her into his arms.

She snuggled close to him, content for now to rest her body against his. "Tired?"

"This has been a heck of a day," he said, caressing her back. He pulled back from her and looked down at her face. "I've got to go out of town tonight."

Disappointment settled in her stomach. She missed him already. "Where? For how long?"

"Nashville. I have to stand in at a principal's retreat for Malcolm. Unfortunately, it's for the entire weekend. I won't be back until Sunday night."

"I guess it can't be helped," she said, feeling selfish for wanting him in town. With her.

"You know what this means, don't you?"

It meant she'd miss him. A lot. Then it dawned on her. "You can't take the boys on their camp-out."

He dropped down on the edge of her desk and pulled her between his legs. "That's right."

"It can't be helped, Dillon," she said, wanting to

ease the anxiety she saw in his eyes. "The boys will understand."

"Right," he said, his face grim. "This will be the first time I've disappointed Glenn. How do you think he's going to take it?"

She sighed. Glenn and Calvin had been talking about this camp-out all week. They'd already gone shopping at the sporting goods store for gear. They'd even had a practice session and slept in their sleeping bags in the house. "I really don't know," she answered honestly. "He's so happy now and he hasn't had any incidents at school. I think he'll be all right."

"I wish I could get out of this. But it's such short notice that I can't get anyone else to fill in for me."

His concern for their son touched her deeply and cemented further the love she felt for him. "It was bound to happen, Dillon. Things come up and Glenn has to learn to accept life's little disappointments." His grim smile didn't fade. "Now, cheer up. You know I'm right. We'll talk to him and Calvin tonight, and we'll camp out next weekend. They'll understand."

"Maybe I could ask Dad or Donald to fill in for me?" The hopefulness in his voice tugged at her heartstrings.

"No, Dillon. Your father and mother have plans for Friday, and you know Donald has a date. This won't kill the boys. We'll do it next weekend. They'll be fine."

He looked at her with uncertain eyes and pulled her into his embrace. "I hope you're right."

She rested her head on his chest. *I hope I am, too,* she thought. *I hope I am, too.*

* * *

Dillon pulled his truck into his parents' driveway right after Monique parked her car. Before either of them could get out of their vehicles, the boys were bounding out the front door and heading their way.

"Look what Grandpa made us," Calvin was saying. Both boys waved what looked like flags. Well, what they held actually looked like a triangular piece of cloth on a thin pole about three feet long.

"Grandpa says this will keep the animals away from the campfire," Glenn explained. "We have four. One for each corner of the yard."

Dillon and Monique each took a flag.

"That's good work," Dillon said, making a production of studying the craftsmanship of the flag. "We'll definitely need these."

"Grandpa really saved us this time," Monique added.

Dillon glanced over the boys' heads at her, then sighed. He stooped down so he'd be eye level with his sons. "I've got some bad news about our camp-out, guys," he said. "We're going to have to postpone it a week."

"Why?" both boys moaned. "We want to go camping."

Dillon felt Monique's hand on his shoulder and took confidence in her support. "I have to go out of town on business, and I won't be back until Sunday. But we can do the camp-out next weekend."

"But you said we'd do it this weekend," Glenn accused.

"Yeah," Calvin added. This time Dillon wished Calvin didn't follow his big brother's lead so readily.

Monique stooped down next to Dillon, keeping her hand on his shoulder. "Next weekend is only a few days away. The time will pass quickly. Plus, you'll be on Thanksgiving vacation, so you'll have more days to camp out."

Dillon studied both boys. Calvin seemed to accept the change in plans, but he clearly waited for his older brother's response before committing himself. Glenn, on the other hand, frowned. Neither boy said anything.

"So what do you say, men?" Dillon asked, trying to keep his tone light.

"Glenn?" Monique urged, when the boy didn't say anything.

Glenn began shaking his head from left to right. "I don't care," he said, his voice shaky. "I don't care." He took the flag he held, broke it across his leg and threw it on the ground. "I don't care." He turned and ran around the house.

"What's wrong with Glenn?" Calvin asked, his voice thick.

Monique pulled the child into her embrace. "Nothing, sweetheart. He's just disappointed about the change in plans. He'll be fine."

The hurt on Dillon's face made Monique want to pull him into her arms and comfort him, as well.

He sighed. "I'll go talk to him."

"Maybe he needs some time to cool off first," Monique offered. "He'll come around, Dillon."

He shook his head. Glenn was his son, and it was time the boy heard some things straight from his father. "No, I think I'll talk to him now."

Monique nodded agreement. "Calvin and I will go inside and talk to your parents."

Dillon stuffed his hands in his pockets and headed around the house after his son. *His son.* He'd waited for Glenn to accept him as a father, and he was willing to wait for as long as it took. But he couldn't let his son go another minute without hearing how much he loved him.

He wasn't surprised to find the boy sitting on a bench in his father's toolshed. Dillon smiled. This was the place he'd gone to pout when he was about Glenn's age. He took a seat next to his son. The boy scooted down the bench and Dillon's heart clogged in his throat. "Glenn, I'm sorry we had to postpone our camp-out. But I have to go out of town on business for the school. We'll have our camp-out next weekend," he said.

"I don't care." Glenn studied the power tools on the back wall of the shed. "Who ever heard of camping out in a yard anyway?"

Dillon wanted to pull Glenn into his arms and hug him until he cried Uncle. But he didn't do it. He was afraid of Glenn's response. Or rather, his lack of response. "Just because I have to postpone our camp-out doesn't mean that I don't love you, Glenn, because I do. I love you very much. No man could be prouder of his children than I am of you and Calvin. I love you both very much, and I really hate to disappoint you. But it can't be helped this time."

"You don't love me," Glenn said, wiping his hand across his face. "My daddy loved me. You're not my daddy."

Dillon felt the pain of Glenn's words deep in his heart, and tears filled his own eyes. "I know Charles loved you, Glenn. And I know you miss him." He leaned forward and rested his elbows on his knees. "I'm so sorry he had to leave you. But he didn't *want* to leave. It was beyond his control. He was sick, and

God took him to a place where he wouldn't be sick anymore. But I'm not leaving you, Glenn. I'm just going on a business trip. I'll be back Sunday."

Dillon waited for Glenn's response to his words, and when, after a few minutes, there was none, he thought there wasn't going to be any. But then Glenn's small shoulders began to shudder, and he knew he'd been wrong. He leaned toward his son then, and did what he'd wanted to do since he'd first met him. He wrapped his big strong arms around him and hugged him with all the love he felt in his heart. Glenn didn't resist. When Dillon felt his small arms go around his waist, the tears he'd been holding in were forced out. Two generations of Bell men sat in the toolshed and wept.

After she and Calvin had entered the house, Monique suggested that he get his things together while she spoke with his grandmother. She quickly told Mrs. Bell of Dillon's change of plans and Glenn's response to them.

"They'll work it out, dear." Mrs. Bell patted Monique on her shoulders. "Don't worry about them. Let me get you something to drink."

Before Monique could respond, the older woman was out of the room and on her way to the kitchen. Monique went to the window and looked out, wondering what was going on between Dillon and Glenn. When Mrs. Bell returned, Monique forced herself away from the window and took the hot tea the older woman had so graciously prepared.

She sipped from the cup then sat down on the couch. Mrs. Bell took the chair next to her.

"How was school today?"

Mrs. Bell's question warmed Monique's heart because she knew the woman was trying to keep Monique's mind off of Glenn and Dillon. She opened her mouth to give Mrs. Bell the generalities of her day and soon found that she was actually enjoying the conversation. She realized that she and Mrs. Bell had developed a sort of friendship, a mutual respect and liking for each other.

"Well, Dillon says you're doing a good job," Mrs. Bell said. "We're proud of you, Monique."

Embarrassed and surprised, Monique waved off the woman's praise. "I'm lucky," she said. "And I work with some great people."

Mrs. Bell was about to respond, but Calvin walked into the room with his backpack and his other belongings. He sat down next to Monique, almost snuggling against her, and she felt his anxiety. With a shy smile to Mrs. Bell, she lifted the young boy onto her lap and hugged him close in her arms. "It's all right, sweetheart. Your daddy and your brother will be in after a while." She pressed a kiss against the top of his head and continued to hold him.

"You're good with him, Monique," Mrs. Bell said.

She smiled down at Calvin. "He's good *for* me," she said, and meant it. She couldn't love Calvin more if he were her natural child. It was as if Calvin and Glenn each filled different places in her heart. She loved them both dearly.

At that moment, Glenn and Dillon entered through the front door. Monique took Dillon's hand on Glenn's shoulder as a good sign. "Why don't you get your things, Glenn, so we can get ready to go?" Dillon said.

Glenn looked up at him, nodded, then left the room to get his things.

Calvin scooted off Monique's lap to follow his brother, but his father stopped him. "How'd you like to spend the night with Grandma while Daddy is out of town?"

Calvin looked at his grandmother, then at Monique. "I want to stay with Moni," he said.

Monique shot a quick glance at Mrs. Bell, wanting to see her response to her grandson's request. She didn't want the older woman to feel that she was taking her place in her grandson's life.

"I think that's a good idea, Dillon," Mrs. Bell said. "The boys need to be together."

Dillon cast a questioning glance at Monique. "Are you up for having both of them?"

"Sure," she said. "We'll have fun, won't we, Calvin?"

The boy's face split into a wide grin. "Yeah. I gotta go tell Glenn." He scampered out of the room in search of his older brother.

After the boy was out of sight, Dillon strode over and dropped down on the couch next to Monique. Though he looked relieved, she felt the tension in him. She wished she were free to turn and take him in her arms.

"What happened?" she and Mrs. Bell asked at the same time.

He shrugged his broad shoulders. "We talked. I think it'll be all right now."

Monique wanted to inquire further, but at Dillon's obvious exhaustion, she decided to leave the topic alone for now.

"I told you they would work it out," Mrs. Bell

said to Monique. She got up. "I baked some cookies. Give me a couple of minutes for them to cool, and I'll bag them up and you can take them home for the boys' dessert tonight."

Monique nodded. After Mrs. Bell left the room, Dillon turned and embraced her. She hugged him tight to her breast and tried to relieve some of his tension. "Do you want to talk about it?" she asked, rubbing her hands up and down his back in a comforting motion.

"Not now. Maybe later. After the boys are in bed."

"But I thought you were leaving tonight."

"I changed my mind. I'll leave first thing in the morning. I'll be a little late, but what the hell."

"Dillon," she admonished. "That's not necessary. I'll take care of the boys."

He pulled back from her. "Yes, it is necessary. I need to be here, Monique. He's my son."

Monique couldn't stop the hurt that immediately surrounded her. "I know that, Dillon."

Dillon shook his head, then pulled her back into his arms. "I'm sorry. I'm not angry with you. I just hate it when they hurt. I'd give my right arm for them not to hurt."

"I know. I feel the same way."

He pulled back again and ran his finger down her jaw. "I know you do. You're a great mother."

"And you're a wonderful father."

"We make a good pair, don't we?"

Monique's breath caught in her throat. They did make a good pair. They were good parents to their two children. All that was missing from this almost-family situation was a committed relationship between her and Dillon. She knew he cared about her, that he enjoyed her company, her conversation and her body. But she didn't know any more because Dillon hadn't revealed any more.

"I need to be with you tonight," he whispered against her ear. "It's been too long."

She felt the same way, but she didn't see how they could manage it with both boys under the same roof with them. "We can't, Dillon."

"I know we can't make love, but there's nothing to stop me from holding you, is there? Can't I hold you tonight, Monique?"

No request could have been sweeter. "All night long, if you want." She pressed closer to him. "Oh, Dillon, I need you, too. So much."

"Shhh..." he said. "Why don't you go get the cookies from Ma and round up the boys while I get myself together?"

She glanced down at his lap. "Oh."

"Yes, oh. Now go."

Monique reluctantly left Dillon and did as he suggested. In no time at all, she'd gotten the boys and the cookies and they were on their way to her house. Once there, she and Dillon quickly prepared a light dinner, which they ate over a subdued but not unhappy table. After dinner, the two of them helped the boys with their schoolwork and then joined them in a couple of rounds of a new video game Glenn had begged her to buy. Finally, the boys' bedtime rolled around and the adults shuffled them off to bed.

Dillon dropped his arm around Monique's shoulder and pulled her close to him as soon as they shut the door to the boys' room. "I love them dearly," he said, "but I thought eight-thirty was never going to come."

She leaned into him and wrapped her arms around his waist. "I know what you mean."

Wrapped in each other's arms, they walked to the family room and sank down onto the overstuffed couch. Dillon immediately pulled Monique onto his lap and began to place caressing kisses down the side of her neck.

She leaned back and enjoyed his touch, thinking life couldn't get much better. Dillon had feelings for her. Deep feelings. She just needed to wait until he was ready to share them. She believed she could last that long.

"Do you have any idea how much I want you?" he asked, his voice hoarse with passion.

She shifted on his lap and the feel of him hard against her forced a moan from her lungs. "I think I have some idea."

He pushed his erection against her.

"We can't, Dillon," she reminded him.

"I know." He placed a hand over her breast. "Just let me touch you. I promise I won't go any further."

His touch, as usual, set off rockets in her. "It's not you I'm worried about," she said.

The chuckle he gave in response was dry. "You have a point there." He pressed her head against his shoulder. "Okay, we'll just sit here. It'll be torture, but I have to hold you."

Chapter Seventeen

Monique and the boys had an active weekend with a trip to the zoo and a movie. She'd offered to let them camp out in her backyard, but they preferred to wait for Dillon to get back. She took that to mean that the troubled waters between Glenn and Dillon had settled. As a matter of fact, Glenn seemed totally okay about the incident.

She didn't know who was happier with Dillon's return on Sunday night—her or the boys. They monopolized his time, giving him a blow-by-blow account of their weekend without him before starting in with endless questions about their upcoming adventure. Monique sat next to Dillon, his fingers teasingly caressing her neck, and she enjoyed the entire evening.

After the boys were in bed and they were alone, Dillon pulled her into his arms. "I missed you," he said. He captured her lips in a kiss that told her how much. When he pulled away, they were both out of breath. "We've got to stop this, you know."

She grinned up at him. "Stop what? Kissing?"

He pulled her closer. "Stop just kissing. We need some time alone."

Monique agreed, but she didn't know where they would find the time. "Any suggestions for how we do that?"

He wiggled his eyebrows. "We could share a sleeping bag during our camp-out."

"And what would we do with the four curious eyes that would be on us all the time?"

He sat down on the couch and pulled her onto his lap. "You sure know how to spoil a fantasy. We could always ask my parents to keep them for a weekend, and we could go somewhere together."

She shook her head. The thought of asking his mother to keep the boys so they could make love made her uncomfortable. "You can't be serious. You'd really ask your mother to keep the boys so we could have a rendezvous? I'd never be able to look the woman in the face again."

He rubbed his chin as if in deep thought. "You have a point. You and Ma are becoming pretty friendly. I guess it would be awkward. What if we asked Donald?"

"I don't think we should ask anybody to keep them. We'll just have to take advantage of any opportunities that present themselves."

"Like we did the weekend after Halloween."

"Exactly."

He grunted. "What if we have to wait until next Halloween before we make love again?"

She smiled, unable to resist teasing him. "I can wait, can't you?"

He didn't bother answering that ridiculous question. He lowered his head and teased her lips with his own. He'd meant the kiss as a challenge to her. She'd said she could wait a year. Well, his plan had been to prove to her that she could no more wait than he could. But somewhere between the plan forming in his mind and his lips pressing against hers, he'd become his own victim.

Dillon wasn't sure he was going to make it through Thanksgiving Day. Every time he looked at Monique, he had to fight the overwhelming urge to throw her over his shoulder, take her someplace and have his way with her. Thank goodness she'd spent most of the morning in the kitchen with his mother, or he'd have made a fool of himself for sure.

He looked up from the football game he was watching on television and took a quick glance at the kitchen door, hoping to get another glimpse of her. Okay, so he was a masochist. He couldn't be around her without wanting her, and she couldn't be out of his sight without him thinking about her. He'd definitely lost control of this relationship.

Donald dropped down on the couch next to him, a bag of freshly roasted peanuts in his hand. His father and the boys were out back roasting them now. "What's up, bro?" he asked, throwing back a couple of peanuts. "You can't stand for her to be out of your sight?"

Dillon didn't want to have this conversation with his brother, so he got up and went out onto the porch.

It was November, so the weather was cool but not yet cold. He sat down on the front porch steps.

The sound of the screen door closing behind him told him Donald had followed him outside. "No need to be rude, man," Donald said. "You can't get away from me anyway. So what's up with you and Monique? And don't tell me nothing because I've got eyes in my head and I know better."

Dillon cut a warning glance at his brother. "If you know so much, why don't you tell me?"

"Well," Donald said, popping more peanuts in his mouth. "I think she's in love with you. The question is, how do you feel about her?"

Dillon's heart slammed against the walls of his chest at his brother's declaration. Monique was in love with him? "And what makes you think Monique is in love with me?"

Donald stuffed more peanuts in his mouth. "I have eyes, man. Anybody can see it from the way she looks at you. Even Ma's noticed it. You've been doing a lot of looking yourself. Have you told her yet that you love her?"

"No," he said. His chest felt tight. "Why would I tell her that?"

"Because it's true?"

"No way. I'm a lot of things, but crazy I'm not. And I'd have to be crazy to fall in love with Monique again."

"There's an asylum down the road. When do you want me to sign you up?"

Dillon cut a glance at his brother. "I think you're the one who needs to go to that asylum."

"Fun-ny. Come off it, Dillon. You love her."

"I think I know my own feelings, Donald."

"So you're telling me that you don't have strong feelings for Monique?"

"That's not what I said. I said I'm not in love with Monique. But I do have feelings for her." Very strong feelings, he added to himself.

"Well, you certainly act like you love her. You spend all your time with her."

"I'm spending time with my son," he said, though he knew he wasn't telling the whole truth. He'd just minutes ago been thinking about his need to be alone with Monique.

"Then why are you always touching her? You can't be in the same room with her without touching her. Tell me why that is."

Dillon didn't have to tell Donald anything, and he decided that he wasn't. What he felt for Monique was strong, but it wasn't love. He wasn't stupid enough to let himself fall in love with her again. No, she'd hurt him too much for him to allow himself to go down that road again.

But he couldn't deny that she still had some hold over him. He'd hoped it was all physical attraction, but he knew it was more. Maybe it was physical attraction coupled with the fact that she was his son's mother. He wasn't sure. He just knew that he enjoyed being with her, enjoyed making love to her, enjoyed seeing her with his boys.

He and Monique had become friends. Okay, they'd become lovers. But they weren't in love. He didn't think she loved him any more than he believed he loved her. They had come together because of the boys. He didn't try to tell himself otherwise. The truth was, had Monique's husband not died, she would not be in his life now and he would never have known his son.

"You say you're not in love with her," Donald said, interrupting his thoughts, "but I don't believe it. But let's put that aside for a minute. She's in love with you, Dillon. It doesn't take a genius to figure that out."

"You're wrong, baby brother. Monique is no more in love with me than I am in love with her."

"Then why have you been sleeping with her?"

Dillon bristled. "Who says I'm sleeping with her?"

"No one had to *say* anything." Donald shook his head. "You're so transparent, brother. I know she was with you the weekend Ma and Daddy took the boys to visit Darnell."

Dillon looked at his brother, his mouth open. He'd been so sure no one had known.

"You really do think I'm stupid, don't you?" Donald said. "Man, if you had looked at that bedroom door one more time that night I came over, I was going to go in there and tell her hello."

"You knew she was with me?"

Donald nodded.

"How'd you know?"

"How could I not? It's in your voice when you talk about her, in your eyes when you look at her. You're happy, Dillon, or you could be, if you'd let yourself. Not many people get the second chance that you and Monique are getting. Don't be stupid and let it slip away."

Donald clapped Dillon on his shoulder. Then he got up and walked into the house, leaving Dillon alone with his thoughts.

He was attracted to Monique, Dillon told himself. He enjoyed her company and he cared about her. But love? He shook his head. He couldn't love her. He was much smarter than that. Wasn't he?

The Bells sat down to Thanksgiving dinner at exactly two o'clock. Mr. Bell's place, now empty, was at one end of the table, Mrs. Bell's at the other, while Dillon and the boys took one side and Monique and Donald, the other. Dillon tried to keep the conversation he'd had with his brother out of his mind, but it wasn't easy with Monique seated across from him. He could barely keep his eyes off her. He might not be in love with her, but she had burrowed under his skin. No doubt about it.

He watched as she leaned over and spoke with his mother. Both women chuckled at the shared secret. They'd become friends and that knowledge caused him deep satisfaction. He looked around the table and realized he had a lot to be thankful for this year. The boys, his parents, his brothers. And Monique. Yes, he was thankful for her. For the courage she'd had in bringing his son back to him.

His father ambled out of the kitchen with the turkey and his big carving knife. After placing the platter on the table, he rubbed the big knife against a big fork, summoning everyone's attention.

"You know I'm not one for speeches," his father said, when everyone looked at him. "But I...actually, we...that's me and my woman down there...just wanted to give thanks for our family. There are three generations of Bell men here today, and we couldn't be happier about it. We have two of our three boys with us and the other one, though he's not here in body, he's in our hearts and we know he's safe." He cleared his throat. "And we're thankful for the third generation of Bell men, Glenn and Calvin. A man couldn't ask for better grandchildren."

"And a woman couldn't ask for better grandsons, either, Daddy," Dillon's mother interjected.

The older man then turned to Monique. "And we're thankful to you, Monique. We're thankful for the care you've taken of our grandson all those years without us, and we're thankful you chose to share him and his love with us. You'll never know how much that means to us."

Dillon watched Monique's eyes fill with tears. He wanted, as he often did, to pull her into his arms. But, of course, he didn't.

"And we're thankful for *you*, Monique," Mr. Bell continued. "You're a good woman, a wonderful mother and just a plain joy to have around. We're glad you're a part of the family, and if we haven't said it before, we say it now. Welcome to the family, sweetheart."

Monique opened her mouth to speak, but tears clogged her throat and choked her words.

"Don't cry, Moni," Calvin said. "We love you."

Monique's tears flowed freely at Calvin's words, but she managed to speak. "I know, sweetheart," she said to Calvin. Then she turned first to Mrs. Bell, then to Mr. Bell. "Thank you both for accepting Glenn and me. Each of you has taken a special spot in our hearts." She wiped her tears with her napkin, then nodded to her son. "Isn't that right, Glenn?"

The nine-year-old nodded. "I'm thankful that I have a grandma, a grandpa, three uncles, an aunt, a little brother, a mom and—" he ducked his head "—a daddy."

Dillon's throat closed up. He wanted to speak, but he couldn't find the words. He reached over Calvin and rubbed Glenn on his head. "And I'm thankful that this year I have two sons," he said with feeling. "This has got to be the best Thanksgiving of my life."

Dillon followed Monique's example and took a napkin to his eyes.

"How come everybody is crying?" Calvin asked, sounding truly bewildered.

Dillon's gaze traveled around the table and he saw that Calvin was right. Everybody was in tears or very close to them.

Donald leaned across the table and said to Calvin in a loud whisper, "I think they're crying because Daddy won't slice the turkey."

Everyone at the table laughed at that ridiculous statement, and the laughter lightened the mood. The solemn part of the day was over and now they could just enjoy each other. Dillon looked across the table to get Monique's attention, but this time she was talking to Donald. If he hadn't known better, he'd think she was avoiding looking at him. But that didn't make any sense.

Well, he said to himself, he and Monique would have their time tonight after the boys were in bed. He couldn't wait.

Monique waited by the front door while Dillon stowed Glenn's camping equipment in the closet. The boys were staying with him tonight since they were camping out tomorrow night and Saturday night.

When he finished, he turned and smiled at her. Any other time, the smile would have had her melting in his arms. But tonight was different. He moved to take her in his arms as he usually did once the boys were in bed, but she stepped away from him.

"Is something wrong?" he asked.

She looked into his eyes, looking for the love that she was so sure she'd seen there. The love that she'd been waiting for him to confess any day now. "No, nothing's wrong," she lied. Everything was wrong. "I'm just tired and I want to go home and get in bed."

"Are you feeling all right?" he asked, sounding truly concerned. "I could get you some aspirin or something."

She shook her head. "No, that won't be necessary. I'll be fine. I just need to get home."

He took another step toward her and again she moved back. "Look, Monique, if you're that tired, you don't need to drive home. You can stay here."

She gave him a look that said he was crazy.

"I'll sleep on the couch and you can sleep in my bed, if that's what you're worried about."

If only it were that simple, she thought. "No, Dillon. I told you, I'm fine. I'll just drive home and get in bed." She turned and opened the door. "See you tomorrow," she said, then walked through the door and to her car.

She felt her mask slipping even as she walked to the car. She just prayed she'd reach the vehicle without making a fool of herself. How could she have been so stupid? She should have known that the Fates would only allow her a measured amount of happiness. What was she doing anyway, thinking she could have it all?

She made it to her car on wobbly legs and with a broken heart. As she slid in, she glanced back and gave Dillon a fake smile. It was the best she could do under the circumstances. She managed to get her key in the ignition and the car in gear. She didn't look at Dillon as she backed out of his drive and onto the street.

Once she turned off his street, her tears began to fall. "I'm not in love with Monique," he'd told his brother. The words sounded loud and garish in her ears, and she knew she'd hear them until the day she died. Dillon didn't love her, and by the tone of voice he'd used he didn't *want* to love her.

She wiped at her face with one hand while gripping the steering wheel with the other. She'd endured so much in her life. So much. And she'd risen above every hardship, every challenge. But she didn't know if she could do it this time. Before, she'd always had Dillon's love to fall back on. Now that crutch was gone.

"I'm not in love with Monique," his voice sounded again, and even the wounded groan that came from her lips couldn't mask the sound.

Chapter Eighteen

Later that night, Monique finished rinsing her coffee cup and placed it in the dishwasher just as the doorbell rang. She closed the door to the dishwasher and headed for the front of the house, wondering who would be visiting at this hour. She was certainly in no mood for company. When she pulled open the door, Donald's smiling face greeted her.

"May I come in?" he asked.

She held on to the door. "It's late, Donald, and I'm not feeling well."

His smile faded and his face turned serious. "You heard us, didn't you? I could see it in your eyes at dinner."

Donald's words went in her ears and down through her lungs, almost suffocating her. He took advantage of her lapse and pushed the door open, letting himself in.

"It's not as bad as it sounded." She stepped back as he pulled the door closed behind him. "Have you spoken to Dillon about it?"

A chill much greater than the mild temperatures would suggest surrounded her, and she wrapped her arms around herself. "Not yet," she said.

"But you're going to, aren't you?"

She turned and walked toward the family room. Donald followed her.

"You are going to talk to him about what you heard, aren't you?" he asked again.

She dropped down onto the couch, followed by Donald. "What's the point, Donald? Dillon was pretty clear in what he said." She wished she could get his words out of her mind, but his "I'm not in love with Monique" kept repeating in her head.

"Dillon was talking crazy, Monique. Even a blind man can see that he's in love with you."

Monique had thought Dillon was falling in love with her again. She'd hoped it. But his very words killed that hope. "Dillon doesn't *want* to be in love with me, Donald. You heard him."

"What I heard was a scared man running away from the best thing that's ever happened to him."

She eyed him skeptically. "Dillon, afraid? You must be joking."

Donald relaxed back into the couch and studied her without speaking.

"Why are you staring at me?" she asked, uncomfortable with his eyes burning into her.

"I'm trying to figure out who's the bigger fool— you or Dillon." He leaned forward. "You know, Monique, I've never been in love. I'm twenty-six years old and I've never been in love. Not really. And sometimes that makes me sad."

Monique didn't know what to say. Donald was never at a loss for female companionship, though now that she thought about it, he hadn't brought any of his dates around to any family gatherings since she'd been back in town.

"But look at you and Dillon," he continued. "You fell in love—real love—in high school. You were separated, but even time and distance didn't destroy the love that was between you. And now that you've found each other again, you're both too stubborn to embrace that love. Instead of Dillon talking about how he doesn't love you and you walking around all hurt because he said it, the both of you should be planning to spend the rest of your lives together. I know that's what I'd be doing." His speech complete, Donald got up from the couch and kissed her on her forehead. "You left him, Monique, so you're going to have to be the one who holds this together. If you don't fight for him, you're gonna lose him because he's too afraid to reach out to you and be left again." He squeezed her shoulder, then left the room. She heard the front door click as he let himself out of the house.

Dillon woke up the next morning with Monique on his mind, so his first action of the day was a phone call to her house.

"Good morning," he said when she answered.

"Dillon?" her sleep-filled voice responded.

"Last time I looked," he said with a smile. He eased down in the bed, wishing she were there with him. "Feeling better this morning?"

"A little," she said. She still heard his painful words, but they didn't stab at her heart as deeply as they had yesterday and last night.

"Are you sure you don't need to go to the doctor?" There had been a hesitancy in her voice that concerned him.

"No," she said, sounding more definite. What she needed was for him to love her. For him to want to love her.

"How about coming over and having breakfast with me and the boys?"

"Ahh, not this morning, Dillon," she hedged. "I want to get in some Christmas shopping since I don't have the boys underfoot. You know the day after Thanksgiving is the biggest shopping day of the year." She hoped her fake cheer satisfied him, because right now she felt anything but happy. Maybe a day of Christmas shopping would help. It definitely couldn't hurt.

"So you're going to spend the day at the malls?" he said with what she thought was disappointment in his voice.

"That's right."

"Am I keeping you?" he asked, a bit of impatience in his voice.

So he was finally getting the message. She'd deliberately kept her responses short in the hope that he would come to that conclusion. "I do have to get to the malls," she said with a lightness she didn't feel. "I don't want all the good gifts to be picked over."

"You're still joining us tonight for the camp-out, aren't you?" He sounded as though he really wanted her answer to be affirmative. Yesterday, she would have believed he did. Today she wasn't so sure.

"Well, I was thinking about that. Maybe you and the boys should do it without me. I don't think they want me there anyway. Not really."

"You have other plans?"

"With the holidays coming and everything, I have a thousand little things to do. You know how that is."

"Yes, I guess I do." His response was terse and she guessed he had lost all patience with her.

"Well, give the boys a kiss for me and tell them I'll see them on Sunday."

Monique stood outside Dillon's front door on Sunday morning, dreading coming face-to-face with him again. Her holiday errand running had been a bust. The knowledge that Dillon didn't want to care for her had kept her lamenting what could have been. Again. Why did it seem her life was going in circles? She'd felt on the verge of having it all only twice in her lifetime. Ten years ago, when she and Dillon had been in love, and the month since she and Dillon had made love on Halloween. And both times, she'd been denied. The first time she'd had the love of her child and memories of Dillon's love to keep her sane. Now, she would have to rely on her love for Glenn and Calvin to keep her sane because Dillon's love was out of reach.

Strengthening her resolve to handle herself with dignity and not show how devastated she was, she reached for the doorbell.

"Let me do that for you, beautiful."

She jumped at the sound of Donald's voice. "I didn't hear you drive up," she said, noticing the black-and-white patrol car now parked behind her vehicle.

"Gotta stop thinking so hard." Donald pulled a key out of his pocket and inserted it into the door. He pushed it open, then waved her in before him. "After you."

"We probably should have knocked, Donald," she said, going in before him.

He gave her a long look, then sighed. "You haven't talked with him, have you?"

"Donald—"

He lifted his hand. "Don't even try to explain. Just consider this your lucky day." He turned from her and walked to the front of the hallway leading to the bedrooms. "Hey," Donald yelled at the top of his lungs. "Where is everybody?"

As if on cue, Glenn and Calvin rushed out of their room and down the short hallway to their uncle. "Uncle Donald," they both said cheerfully. Then, seeing her back near the foyer, they added, "Moni." "Mom."

"Are you going camping with us next time?" Glenn asked Donald, who had picked Calvin up and was holding him over his head.

"Not me," Donald said, placing the boy back on the floor. "I like sleeping in my nice, firm bed. Camping is for you outdoor types."

The boys seemed genuinely pleased by that answer.

"Hey, how'd you guys like a ride in my patrol car?"

"No, Donald," Monique interrupted, understanding the man's plan. "There's no need for you to do that. You must have to get to work."

"Aw, Mom," Glenn said.

Donald shook his head. "No problem. I have permission from the chief to give these two big guys a tour of the town." He rubbed Glenn's head. "How about it, men?"

"Yay," both boys said, clapping their hands.

"Are we going now?" Calvin asked.

"Right now. You guys get your jackets."

"Okay," they said and rushed out of the room.

"Hey, hey, slow down." Dillon almost bumped into the boys when he came out of the bathroom. "Where's the fire?"

"Uncle Donald is taking us for a ride in his police car," Glenn said. "We've got to get our jackets."

"Yeah," Calvin added. "We have to get our jackets."

As if that were explanation enough, the boys rushed off to their bedroom.

Dillon glanced down the hall at Monique and Donald. "What was that all about?"

"I'm taking them for a ride in the patrol car," Donald said. When Dillon joined them in the foyer, Donald clamped an arm around his older brother's head. "Are you deaf or something? They told you what we were going to do."

Monique watched the brothers with a heavy heart. Though Dillon pushed at Donald's arm and chastised him, his love for his brother was evident in his eyes. She'd seen love of another kind in his eyes when he looked at her. But looks weren't enough for her.

"Monique, this guy is a wimp," Donald said to her. "I don't know what you see in him."

Monique didn't know what to say, so she said nothing.

Dillon finally broke out of Donald's hold. "Morning, Monique. Ignore my brother here. He's reverting to his childhood." Dillon glanced at his brother. "Then again, maybe he never left his childhood."

"We're ready," the boys said as they bounded back into the room. "Let's go." They each grabbed one of Donald's hands and began pulling him to the door.

"I guess we're leaving," Donald said with a crooked smile. "The natives are restless."

Monique smiled. Regardless of how hurt she was that things weren't going to work out for her and Dillon, she was happy for the life her son had found. "Have fun, guys," she said, feeling better about the day.

"We will, Mom," Glenn said.

"Okay, Moni," Calvin said.

Monique looked at Dillon. "I guess I'll be going, too," she said as they watched the boys lead Donald to the police car.

Dillon pushed the front door closed with one hand and tugged at her arm with the other. "Don't go. We don't get much time alone. Let's take advantage of this."

The caress in his voice and the glint in his eyes worked together to make her forget what she'd heard yesterday. Almost. "I don't think that's such a good idea, Dillon."

He pulled her into his arms and touched his lips to hers for a kiss. She wanted so much to give in to her feelings for him, but she knew doing so would only prolong the agony. Using willpower she didn't know she had, she kept her mouth closed and resisted the primitive urge to yield to him.

He pulled back. "What's wrong?" he asked, concern in his eyes.

She stepped away from him. The temptation to give in to her feelings for him was greater the closer she was to him. "What are we doing, Dillon?"

He gazed into her eyes and she was forced to look away. "I thought we decided. We're in a relationship."

"I know," she said, feeling foolish and insecure and so very much in love. "But to what end? What do you want out of this relationship?"

"What do most people want out of a relationship?" He rubbed his hand across his head—a gesture of frustration, she knew.

"But we aren't most people, Dillon," she said softly. "We have a history, and we have a child together."

He moved away and leaned against the wall. "I know, Monique. I know."

She swallowed. It was now or never. "Are you falling in love with me again, Dillon?"

Dillon opened his mouth, but no words came out. He closed it.

Monique fought back the tears that were destined to fall. "I guess that settles it." She took a deep breath. "I need to go shopping."

She turned and took confident steps to the door. "Wait a minute, Monique," he called to her. "Can't we talk about this some more? I just need some time."

Monique didn't turn around. She couldn't. She couldn't put herself through any more secret moments of shared passion. Not only didn't Dillon love her, he didn't *want* to love her. The former she could handle because she could hope that, in time, he'd come to love her. But the latter truth defeated her.

"I'll be by later to pick up Glenn," she said. She opened the door and walked out of the house and away from the man she'd loved all her life.

Dillon stared at the door as it closed behind Monique. He knew she wanted him to tell her that he loved her, but he wasn't ready to make that kind of commitment. To give her that kind of power over him. Not yet.

As he continued to stare at the door, his heart beat faster in his chest. You'll make her understand, he told himself. Just give it some time.

But he wasn't so sure he was right. The hurt in her eyes told him that she was closing her heart to him. He quickly opened the door and rushed out after her.

"Monique," he called to her. Already in her car, she looked up at him. His heart hurt at the tears that he saw streaming down her face as he approached her. Had someone else put those tears there, he'd be out looking for them now to give them a piece of his mind and maybe even his backhand. But how did he backhand himself?

He pressed his hand against her window just as she started the car. "Please, Monique," he said. "Let's talk about this." She looked at him again. "Please."

She rolled down the window and turned off the ignition. He opened her door so she could get out, but she didn't move. He stooped down next to her. "Are you in love with me, Monique?" he asked softly.

She looked into his eyes and he saw the anger behind her tears. She loved him and he'd known it. But it had been easier not to deal with the emotion.

"I love you, too," he said, the words awkward on

his lips. It had been a long time since he'd told a woman he loved her. In his experience, that declaration had been a losing game.

"You don't have to say the words, Dillon," she replied with a sad smile on her face.

But he did have to say it. He had to say it so he could come to grips with what it meant. "It's true," he said. "I guess I've never stopped loving you."

Monique shook her head slowly from side to side and her lips turned down in a larger frown. "Loving somebody should make you happy, Dillon. What you feel isn't love."

"How do you know what I feel?" he asked, insulted by her rejection of his affection. "You've never known how I felt. If you had, we wouldn't be in this situation now."

"What's that supposed to mean?" Her tears dried up and her eyes flashed her anger.

"You know what it means. You want me to love you, to feel good and happy about loving you. But look what loving you in the past has done for me, Monique? I have a nine-year-old son whom I've only known for three months."

"But I explained that, Dillon. You—"

He shook his head. He didn't want to hear her excuses now. "It doesn't matter what your reasons were. What matters is how you chose to handle *our* problem. And it was our problem, Monique."

"That's exactly the reason I didn't tell you. Glenn wasn't a problem for me. He was a baby. A baby born of the love I felt for you. But I knew that's the way you'd see him, the way you'd see me. I knew it and I couldn't bear it. I couldn't." Her tears were back now. "It would have killed me."

"So you chose to kill me, instead?" That got her attention and her eyes again flashed at him. "How do you think I felt when you left? When I tracked you down and found you married and pregnant? All that was beyond my experience, Monique. My experience told me that when people loved each other, they stayed together and worked things out. That's what my parents did. And that's what I thought we'd do. But you just walked away. Just walked away." Dillon felt the hurt as if it were that day ten years ago when he'd gone looking for her. "Something inside me died that day, Monique. I became a shadow of the person I was meant to me. I can love my parents. I can love my brothers. I can love my boys. And loving each of them fills me up. But loving you? You're right. Loving you isn't something I relish, because I know firsthand what it means to love you, Monique. I've got the scars to prove it."

When he stopped talking, he knew he'd said too much, but he also knew he'd spoken from his heart. He waited for her response.

"So this is where we are," she said softly, defeated. "You can't forgive me. You can't separate the scared girl I was then from the woman I am now." She started the ignition. "Maybe you're not in love with me at all, Dillon. Maybe you're still in love with your high school sweetheart." She shook her head. "And that's a shame. We could have had the family and the life we both want." She reached for the car door and pulled it to her, forcing him to move away from her.

"Maybe it would be better if you had Donald drop Glenn off at home," she said. "We could probably use the time apart." She put the car in gear and backed out of the driveway without waiting for his response.

Dillon was sitting on his front steps an hour later when Donald returned with the boys. Glenn and Calvin dropped down on either side of him and regaled him with tales of their drive in the police car while his brother stood, looking down at him with questioning eyes.

"Can we go get our sleeping bags out again?" Glenn asked, after the fifth telling of the half-hour trip.

Dillon had to smile at the boy's eagerness. "You want to use the sleeping bags in the daytime?"

"It'll be fun, Daddy," Glenn said. "We can do it by ourselves. We don't need a fire or anything. We'll just put the sleeping bags out in the backyard the way we did yesterday."

Dillon studied their eager faces, then grinned. "Go ahead. Take my bag out, too. I'll be out there in a minute."

"All right," Glenn said. He turned to Calvin. "Let's get this party started," he said and both boys ran into the house.

"They're sure excited about this camping out bit, aren't they?" Donald asked.

"They're boys," Dillon said, distracted. "What do you expect?"

Donald dropped down on the stoop next to his brother. "Then why do you look like you just lost your dog, or maybe I should say your woman. What did you say to Monique?"

"Not enough, obviously," he said, though in actuality he'd probably said too much. "You know, I don't understand women."

Donald shrugged. "Who does? What does it matter anyway since you don't have to understand them to love them. Even I know that much."

"You do, do you?" Dillon said with skepticism.

Donald leaned back on his elbow. "Of course. While you've been moaning your lost loves, I've been doing some self-study."

"Self-study?" Dillon raised a questioning brow. "I'm not sure I want to hear this."

"You see, Dillon, while you've been shying away from the lovely women of Elberton, I've spent my time compensating for your neglect. It's kept me pretty busy, too."

Dillon grunted. "Sounds like a tough job. I don't see how you were able to do it."

"Well," Donald said with a wide grin, "I take my obligations seriously." His grin relaxed. "But seriously, Dillon. You're making a mistake with Monique. She's the one and you're gonna blow it if you don't wake up."

"I'm not so sure about that, brother. Maybe some love is destined to be left in the past."

"So you're saying that you see a future without Monique?"

The thought unsettled him. "No, I don't. We share the boys. She'll always be a part of my life."

"Wake up, Dillon! What kind of life is that for you or for Monique? She needs something or someone more than the boys, even if you don't."

Dillon didn't feel he needed anyone when he and Monique were together. All he needed was her. Why couldn't she let them progress as they were? Maybe in time—

"You know," Donald continued. "Monique's an attractive woman. Just watch the line form at her door as soon as she makes it known that she's available."

Dillon didn't like the thought of Monique with other men. He didn't like it one bit. But what could he do about it?

Donald got up and brushed off the seat of his pants. "I've got to get this car back," he said. "But do me a favor, brother. Think long and hard about why you're throwing away Monique's love. You may not get another chance with her."

Chapter Nineteen

Monique stood back and watched as Dillon and the boys decorated her and Glenn's Christmas tree. Dressed in his thigh-hugging jeans, a red-and-white pullover that accentuated his broad chest and a matching red-and-white elf hat, Dillon looked like a perfectly contented family man. How she wished she were a part of that family! Being with Dillon and the boys like this was wonderful and at the same time torturous. Every time she looked at Dillon, she thought about how happy they could have been together and how miserable she'd been without him.

The weeks since their breakup had been almost unbearable. Her love for Calvin and Glenn and the knowledge that they needed her had given her the strength to endure her loss. And it *was* a loss. If only Dillon were willing to give them a chance at real happiness.

But Dillon wanted the relationship on his terms and she wasn't willing to live with those terms. How could she be with a man who didn't want to love her and who didn't trust her? She couldn't. She'd spent too many years of her life fighting the spoken words that told her she wasn't good enough, wasn't wanted. She wouldn't spend the rest of her life in a relationship where love wasn't freely given and freely enjoyed. No, she wanted to love, and she wanted to be loved. She wouldn't—couldn't—settle for less.

In spite of her resolve, looking at Dillon now made her wonder about the wisdom of her decision. Silly elf hat and all, he was the man she would love for the rest of her life. She knew already there was no need to talk about getting over him. She wouldn't. Fate had doomed her to loving a man who didn't want to love her. That kind of love wasn't the kind you got over.

"Hey, Mom, look at this." Glenn sat on Dillon's shoulders, pointing at the star that he'd placed atop the tree. "Isn't it great?"

She smiled at the joy on her son's face. His joy and Calvin's would give her the strength to withstand the pain of losing Dillon. "It's wonderful. You guys did a great job."

"Look at this, Moni." Calvin pointed to a peppermint candy cane with a red ribbon bow about its neck. "I made it myself."

She walked over and hugged the adorable Calvin to her side. "That's beautiful, sweetie. We'll have to keep that one until next year."

Calvin beamed at her words. "Did you see it, Daddy?"

Dillon lowered Glenn to the floor and Monique had

to force her eyes not to stare at him. "Sure did, sport." The soft timbre of his voice tickled her senses. She imagined it always would. "I hope you made some special ornaments for the tree at home."

"I made four of them," he said, holding up four fingers.

"Do you have a star for your tree?" Glenn asked.

Calvin looked at his father. "Do we have a star, Daddy?"

"Hmm, we had one." Dillon stroked his chin in an exaggerated fashion as if he were trying to remember. "But I can't remember if I packed it up."

Glenn beamed. "If you don't have one, I'll make you one. I made that one, didn't I, Mom?"

Monique rubbed her son's head as her heart filled with joy. Glenn now had a father, and he was thriving in his father's love. "You sure did."

"Well," Dillon said, looking at Calvin, "what do you think about us forgetting that old star and using the one Glenn made."

Calvin nodded. "We can use my candy canes and Glenn's star." He looked at Monique. "Did you make something, Moni?"

Monique shook her head. "Not me. I think you and Glenn are the talented ones in this family."

"Not so fast there, Monique," Dillon interrupted. "Maybe you don't have talent, but I do." He reached for his jacket, which was lying across the sofa, and tugged out a rectangular box wrapped in green foil. "I've been waiting for just the right moment to hang my handmade ornament." He gave Monique a timid smile that made her heart do a somersault. "Look at this, boys."

Glenn took the ornament and held it so he and Calvin could see. "Wow, Daddy," he said. "It has our names on it and everything. This is so cool. An ornament with our names on it."

Monique looked over Glenn's shoulder and sure enough each side of the rectangle had one of their names. She looked up at Dillon. "When did you do this?"

He shrugged, looking so much like the young boy she'd first fallen in love with that she had to fight back tears. She was going to have to deal with these "almost" family get-togethers much better. Tomorrow night she and Glenn were going to Dillon and Calvin's house to decorate their tree, and then the four of them were spending the next night, Christmas Eve, at Dillon's parents' house. She couldn't spend each night bemoaning their failed love. Somehow she would have to cope, if only for the boys' sake.

"I made it when I went on that school trip to Nashville right before Thanksgiving," Dillon said in answer to her question. "I had some time on my hands so I made good use of it."

Dillon was definitely the sweetest man she knew. And while he told himself that he didn't love her, she knew he felt deeply for her and that love would come if only he would allow it. Just looking at that ornament with their four names on it told her she was right. Dillon already thought of them as a family. Why couldn't he open his heart and allow himself to love her?

"Let me hold it," Calvin said to Glenn. "I want to see my name."

Monique watched as big brother handed the ornament to little brother. "Mom," Glenn said, "now you have to make something. Maybe you could bake some cookies."

Monique heard Dillon's choked laughter and she shot him a stern glance. "You obviously haven't had that talk with them about men's and women's roles, have you?"

"It's on my list of things to do," he said, his shoulders shaking with restrained laughter.

"Well, put it at the top of your list." She could almost forget they were no longer involved when he was laughing and teasing as he was now. Why, she asked herself again, couldn't he allow himself to love her?

"I'll help you, Moni," Calvin said, interrupting her thoughts. "We learned to make a lot of different ornaments at school."

Monique stooped down next to the little boy and gave him a warm hug. "Thank you so much, sweetheart," she said. "But you guys gave special ornaments that you made yourself, and I want to do the same."

"Mom." Glenn rested his hand on her shoulder and she looked up at him. "I'm hungry. When are we going to eat?"

Again, she heard Dillon's titter of laughter. She glanced briefly at him, then turned her attention back to Glenn. "Ask your father," she said. "He's in charge of dinner tonight."

Monique felt quite proud of herself when Dillon's smile faltered just a tad. "Gotcha!" she mouthed.

Dillon watched Monique pull Calvin into a warm embrace, as she often did. It was hard for him to believe that a few months ago he'd questioned the sincerity of her emotions toward the boy. Well, he had no doubts now. Now, he envied the relationship his son shared with Monique.

It seemed forever since Monique had touched him, really touched him. And he missed it. He missed sneaking sweet kisses from her, sharing secret glances with her and spending quiet time with her cuddled on his lap. He missed Monique.

He moved closer to the seven-foot tree that Calvin and Glenn had picked out, a tree almost identical in size and shape to the one they'd decorated last night. The subtle scent of Monique's fragrance enticed him, and he moved closer to her. As if feeling his presence, she turned and smiled at him. The wattage in her smile gave no indication of the state of their relationship. No, her smile said she was happy and content. That everything in her life was just dandy.

Well, everything in his life wasn't dandy and it was all her fault. Why couldn't she give him the time he needed? He didn't say that he would *never* love her. He'd just said that he needed time.

"Daddy," Calvin said, stopping his thoughts. "It's time to put the star on now."

"All right, sport. I guess it is time."

"Here it is." Glenn handed him a star identical to the one Glenn had placed atop the tree at Monique's house last night.

"You're good at this star-making, Glenn." Dillon brushed his hand across his son's head, happy for the freedom to touch him and to love him. His relationship with his son had blossomed and enriched his life greatly since the mishap with the postponed camping trip. He and Glenn were now father and son in all the ways that mattered. "This one looks like you pulled it right out of the sky."

Glenn kicked his sneaker against the living-room carpet. "It's not that good," he said.

"Oh, yes it is." He tilted the boy's chin up. "I know these things. I'm your father."

The boy grinned then. "Aw, Daddy."

"Come on," Dillon said. "Let's get this star on the tree."

"Calvin's gonna do this one, aren't you, Calvin?" Glenn said.

The younger boy's eyes widened and he reached his hands up to his father. Dillon stooped down so that Calvin could climb on his back. Then he stood up and shifted the boy to a comfortable and safe seat on his shoulders. "Ready, sport?" he asked.

"Ready," Calvin said. "Give me the star."

Dillon took the star from Glenn and handed it to Calvin. He glanced at Monique and was surprised to find her teary-eyed. "What's wrong?" he mouthed.

She just shook her head and waved away his attention. Then he understood. Her tears were a mother thing. The smallest thing the boys did moved her to tears. He'd thought since first seeing her with Glenn that she was a wonderful mother. And she had done nothing to make him change his mind. If anything, her actions since then had shown her to be even more wonderful than he'd first thought. And he wasn't the only one who felt this way. Obviously, Calvin and Glenn did, too. So did his parents and Donald. Yes, it was pretty much agreed that Monique wasn't lacking in the parenting department.

"Cut the lights, Mom," Glenn said after Calvin

had secured the star in place. "Let's see how the tree looks in the dark."

While Monique stepped back to flip the light switch, Dillon lowered Calvin to the floor and reached for the plug for the Christmas lights.

"Ready?" Monique asked.

"Ready," Dillon answered. A second after the lights went out, he plugged the Christmas lights' cord into the socket.

"Wow," Glenn said.

"Yay," Calvin added. "Look at our tree, Moni."

Dillon turned in Monique's direction and beckoned her to join him and the boys at the tree. She moved gracefully toward them and stood behind Calvin, her hands on his shoulders.

"It's beautiful, boys."

Glenn, who stood in front of Dillon, said, "All we need now are presents."

"Yeah, when is Santa Claus coming?"

"Tomorrow night, sport," Dillon said. "You know that."

"Why does he have to take so long to come?" Calvin complained. "We've been waiting all year."

Dillon turned and queried Monique with a smile.

"Don't look to me for help. I know how he feels. I can hardly wait for Santa to come myself," she said.

Dillon chuckled. "And what is Santa bringing you?" he asked.

"I don't know what Santa's bringing, but I think two good little boys have been shopping for me." The boys looked up at her and she looked down at them. "I sure wish I knew what they bought me."

"It's a secret," Calvin said.

"Yeah, Mom, you know we can't tell you." Glenn

turned to Calvin and said in a loud whisper, "Mom is like this every year. She always wants to know what her gift is, but we never tell her."

Dillon looked again at Monique and felt a sharp pang of regret at the Christmases he'd not shared with her. He remembered her being childlike about the holiday. She'd always been excited about the smallest gifts, seeming to take pleasure in the unwrapping as much as in the gift itself.

"Hey, Mom," Glenn said. "Where's your ornament? I thought you were making one."

"I am," Monique said. "It's just taking a little longer than I expected. I'll have it tomorrow night at your grandparents'."

"Who's cooking tonight?" Glenn asked. "I'm hungry."

"Tell me something new," Dillon said. "You're always hungry these days."

Glenn grinned. "I'm a growing boy. I have to eat to grow big and strong, don't I, Mom?"

Monique hugged her son to her. "You sure do, Glenn." She looked at Calvin. "I'm hungry, too. How about you?"

Calvin nodded. "Pizza, I want pizza!"

"Yeah, pizza," Glenn agreed.

Monique shot Dillon a quick glance. "You got off easy tonight. You don't have to cook."

He chucked her under her chin, grateful for an excuse to touch her. "I've got to have that talk with the boys before you turn me into a full-time chef."

"Maybe you should try learning to cook something other than lasagna," she suggested saucily.

He stared into her eyes and saw the depth of love in them. He wondered if some of that love belonged to him still, or if she'd redirected all of it to the boys. "Maybe I need a woman to cook for me," he quipped, then left the room to call the pizza delivery service. He picked up the phone thinking that maybe he did need a woman to cook for him.

Mrs. Bell pulled Monique into a firm hug. "Thank you, Monique. It's a wonderful gift." She pulled away and looked back at her husband who held the clay Christmas-bell mobile, with the Bell family names on each bell, that Monique had given the family as a gift. "You've got to hang it up, Daddy. Where are we going to put it?"

"We should put it on the tree, Grandma," Glenn said. "It's a Christmas-tree ornament."

Mrs. Bell patted her hand on her grandson's cheek. "This one is a bit too big for the tree, sweet boy. Your grandpa will have to find a special place to hang it."

Glenn turned to his mother. "But you were making an ornament for the tree, weren't you, Mom?"

Monique brushed her hand across his head. "It started that way, but your grandmother's right, it's a bit too big for the tree."

Mr. Bell scratched his chin. "I have an idea for what I can do," he said. "Yeah, I know exactly what I can do."

"What you gonna do, Grandpa?" Calvin asked.

"Well, I'm going to make a hanger for it, and then I'm going to hook the hanger to the ceiling and let the bells hang from it. It's a big job, though. I'm going to need some help if I'm going to get it finished before Christmas." Mr. Bell looked at his watch. "It's seven o'clock already. I only have five hours."

"We'll help you, Grandpa," Glenn offered. He poked Calvin in the side with his elbow. "Won't we, Calvin?"

"Please, Grandpa, let us help."

"Well, come on. We've got to get started. It'll be your bedtime soon."

Glenn turned to Monique. "We can stay up later tonight, can't we, Mom?"

"Just a little, Glenn. You and Calvin have to be in bed and asleep if you want Santa to come by for a visit."

Glenn turned to his grandfather. "We'll be finished before then, won't we, Grandpa?"

"If we stop talking and get to working, we'll probably have it done."

"We'd better get started, then," Glenn said. "What do we do?"

"First thing," Mr. Bell said, "we get out to the toolshed and look for the right kind of hook." Mr. Bell put a hand on each child's shoulder and turned them toward the kitchen. "Let's get to it."

Monique watched with a happy heart as the three of them walked out of the room.

"The old man still has a way with kids," Donald said. He had left the room briefly to take a phone call and had returned without Monique's hearing him.

"He had enough practice," Dillon added.

"You have a point there, big brother," Donald agreed. He stepped over to the coffee table and picked up the Christmas bells. "There's something wrong with these bells, Monique."

She turned and looked at the mobile, then at Donald. "What's wrong with them?"

"Well," Donald began, studying her handiwork.

"You have Mom and Dad on the top level. That's right. Then you have me, Dillon and Darnell on the second level attached to Mom and Dad. And that's right. But then you go wrong."

Monique looked at the mobile again. "How? I've got Glenn and Calvin on the next level attached to Dillon." She looked up at Donald. "What's wrong with that?"

"You left yourself out."

Monique shot a quick glance at Dillon, who wore a curious expression on his face. Not happy. Not sad. She really couldn't describe it. She turned to Donald and was about to speak, but Dillon spoke first.

"Will you give us a minute, Donald?" he said. "I need to talk to Monique about something."

Donald grinned. A full, wide grin that showed each and every one of his teeth. "It's about time you came to your senses." He clapped his brother on the back, surprised Monique with a quick kiss on the cheek, then left the room, whistling.

"What's wrong with him?" Monique asked, bewildered by Donald's actions. "And what was he talking about?"

Dillon moved to the table and picked up the mobile. He fingered the Christmas bell with his name on it. "He's right. Why didn't you add a bell for yourself?"

"Look at the name on the top, Dillon. It says Christmas *Bells*."

Dillon fingered the square box above his parents' names. Christmas Bells was written in raised, red lettering. "I know what it says."

"I'm not a Bell, Dillon. In case you hadn't noticed."

He stared at her. She still couldn't read his expression and his staring made her uncomfortable. "But you're Glenn's mother, and you're the closest thing to a mother Calvin has ever had. You deserve to be right there next to me."

Monique swallowed. Why was he making her go through this again? What she wanted more than anything in the world was to be right there next to Dillon. As his mate, his friend, his lover, his wife. But that wasn't her role, and showing it on the mobile would have been a lie. The family environment that she and Dillon provided was for the boys. The sad reality was that she was not a Bell and never would be. "I'll make another mobile with me and boys," she said.

He put the bells down then and walked over to her. "That's not what I meant."

She stepped away from him and stared at the Christmas tree they'd decorated. This one was much bigger than the one at her house and the one at Dillon's. And this one had wrapped gifts underneath.

Dillon walked up behind her. He was so close, she could feel the heat of his body against her, though he wasn't touching her.

"I'm a fool, Monique," he whispered. "A damn fool. Please forgive me."

Monique stepped out of Dillon's space, then turned and faced him. "You have done nothing that requires forgiveness, Dillon."

His lips turned down in a grim smile. "Ah, but I have. Like the other day when I told you I didn't want to love you."

She heard his words in her ears and had to suck in her breath again. "Never be sorry for being honest,

Dillon. In that case, honesty was definitely the best policy."

"It may be the best policy, but sometimes it hurts to be honest with the person you love. Especially when you know the truth will hurt them."

Monique nodded. That sentiment she understood. That was how she'd felt when she was pregnant. She'd known that telling Dillon the truth would have, in the long run, hurt him. She wondered if he understood that now.

"I was wrong, Monique. What I should have said was that I already loved you, but that I was afraid to let you know how much."

"But why, Dillon?" she cried. "Don't you think I'm worth loving?"

He pulled her into his arms then, and she collapsed against him. "Sweetheart, you're more than worth it." He stepped back and her head lifted from his shoulder. "And I'm going to spend the rest of our lives showing you how much."

Monique felt hope spring up in her, but she was too afraid to give in to it. "What are you saying, Dillon?"

"I'm saying that I love you. I love you very, very, much. And I want to spend the rest of my life with you, Calvin and Glenn. That is, if you'll have me. I love you, Monique, and I always have. Will you marry me?"

Yes! Yes! Yes! The words rang out in Monique's head, but she couldn't voice them. "Are you sure, Dillon? This seems so sudden. Just the other day you were saying you needed time."

He cupped her face in his hands. "I just told you

how big a fool I was, Monique. I love you. Hell, I've always loved you."

"But—"

"But nothing. I regret that you lied to me about Glenn. I regret that you felt a need to run. But the anger and the hurt is gone. When I look at you now, all I see is love. Your love for the boys. Your love for me. My love for the boys. My love for you. Donald told me once that we were lucky to have a second chance. He was right, Monique. I don't want to lose you again."

Monique still didn't speak. What she wanted most in the world was within her grasp, but she didn't seem to be able to reach for it. Maybe this was all a dream and if she reached for the love Dillon offered, she'd wake up.

"You do love me, don't you, Monique?"

The uncertainty in his voice touched her, giving her the courage to look into his eyes for what she so wanted to see. And there it was. Love, plain and simple. And an uncertain smile that seemed to fear that love being rejected. He did love her! "I've never stopped loving you, Dillon."

Dillon gave a deep sigh. "You had me scared for a minute there. Now why don't you kiss me? I really do need to kiss you."

Monique didn't have to be asked twice. She threw herself into Dillon's arms and kissed him with all the love she'd been forced to keep to herself.

"It's about time," she heard Donald say in the background.

"I knew Dillon was a good son," Mrs. Bell said.

Mr. Bell cleared his throat. "It's a good thing I left the boys on the back porch. I don't think they're old enough for a show like this. I don't even think I'm old enough."

"Let's give them some privacy," Mrs. Bell said.

"I'm with you, Ma," Mr. Bell said. "Come on, Donald."

"Do I have to leave? It's just getting interesting."

"Come on here, boy," Mr. Bell said. "You need to start looking for your own woman."

Dillon broke the kiss and looked down into her eyes. "You know this nosy, loving family comes with me. Do you think you'll be able to handle them?"

There was no doubt in her mind. She looked forward to living in the Bell family circle and told him so.

He nodded, love shining in his eyes. "Good. Now let's get back to the kissing. We have a lot of time to make up for."

Monique opened her mouth for his kiss. She and Dillon had a second chance and a future. This time she had beat fate. She'd held out for the love she knew she deserved. She would never be afraid of fate again. Together she and Dillon could face anything.

Epilogue

Monique was about as happy as a woman could be. She and Dillon would celebrate their first anniversary on New Year's. His Christmas Eve proposal last year had been followed by a quiet family wedding on New Year's Day, with his parents, brothers, their two boys and Sue and her husband in attendance.

They'd had a great year together, and she knew the coming year would be as good if not better. She rested her hand across her now-flat, but soon-to-be expanding stomach. They were going to have a baby. She'd only found out a few days ago and wanted to give Dillon the news as a Christmas present. She was sure he'd be as happy as she was.

"What are you doing out here all alone, sweetheart?" Dillon asked when he walked out on the back porch of his parents' house and joined her. "Aren't you cold?" he asked, wrapping her in his arms.

"Not now." She leaned back in his arms and accepted the warmth he offered. "You always make me hot."

Dillon kissed the side of her neck. "And one day you're going to get in trouble for flirting with me in my parents' house."

She turned in his embrace and smiled up at him. "Promises, promises."

"I'll give you a promise," he said, then kissed her with a passion that left her wanting more. "Just wait until we get home tonight. You're going to get it."

"I'd better," she said.

He grinned down at her. "Have I told you lately how much I love you?"

He had, but she never tired of hearing the words from him. "I could stand hearing it again."

"I love you, Mrs. Monique Bell." He punctuated each word with a soft kiss to her lips. "And I'll always love you."

"I guess you'll have to since you added my name to the Christmas Bells with Krazy Glue. You can't get away from me now."

He chuckled. "The boys helped me. That was the only glue we could find. But I did think it was appropriate."

"Uh-huh."

He pulled back and looked at her. "What are you really doing out here? You're missing all the fun inside. Ma is holding your ornament and telling Darnell and Donald that they need some attachments to their bells. It's driving them crazy."

"I bet it is," she said, with a knowing smile. "And I bet your mother's using you as the example for them to follow."

"Not quite. Ma thinks that maybe we need to think about another Bell. She seems to think that Bell men have sons in threes."

Monique leaned back in his embrace so she could look up at him. "And what do you think, husband?"

Dillon grinned, then captured her lips in a sweet kiss. When he pulled back, he said, "I think I could go for three sons. But only if I get three daughters to go along with them."

Monique's heart swelled with pleasure and she chuckled. "Would it be okay if we started with one?"

Dillon stared into her eyes, and as he read her secret, he dropped his gaze to her stomach. "Are we?" he asked, awe in his voice.

She nodded and her eyes filled with tears when he rested his palm gently against her stomach. This was what she'd missed the first time: seeing the joy in Dillon's eyes at the news that he was going to become a father. She pressed her hand against his jaw. "I love you, Dillon Bell."

He kissed her open palm. "And I love you, Monique Bell. More than you'll ever know."

Monique didn't have the words to tell Dillon how much his love meant to her, so she resolved in her heart to show him each and every day of their lives together. "Come on, perfect husband," she said, removing his hand from her stomach and taking it in her own. "Let's get back to the party. I have a feeling this is going to be a Christmas we won't forget."

* * * * *

Silhouette Desire

THE ELLIOTTS
Mixing business with pleasure

The saga continues this February with

Taking Care of Business
by
Brenda Jackson

They were as different as night and day. But that wouldn't stop Tag Elliott from making it his business to claim the only woman he desired.

Available this February from Silhouette Desire.

Visit Silhouette Books at www.eHarlequin.com

SDTCOB0206

HARLEQUIN Blaze

If you loved
The DaVinci Code,
Harlequin Blaze brings you
a continuity with just as many
twists and turns and,
of course, more unexpected
and red-hot romance.

Get ready for The White Star continuity coming January 2006.

This modern-day hunt is like no other....

Silhouette Desire

This January a new dynasty begins....

THE ELLIOTTS

Mixing business with pleasure

Billionaire's Proposition
by
Leanne Banks

Wealthy playboy Gannon Elliott will do anything to get Erika Layven working for his company again...including giving her the baby she so desperately craves!

Don't miss the exciting launch of a brand-new family dynasty...
THE ELLIOTTS, available every month from Silhouette Desire starting January 2006!

Visit Silhouette Books at www.eHarlequin.com

SDBP0106

HARLEQUIN® Super Romance

HOME TO LOVELESS COUNTY
Because Texas is where the heart is.

MORE TO TEXAS THAN COWBOYS

by Roz Denny Fox

Greer Bell is returning to Texas for the first time since she left as a pregnant teenager. She and her daughter are determined to make a success of their new dude ranch—and the last thing Greer needs is romance, even with the handsome Reverend Noah Kelley.

On sale January 2006

Also look for the final book in this miniseries
The Prodigal Texan (#1326) by Lynnette Kent
in February 2006.

Available wherever Harlequin books are sold.

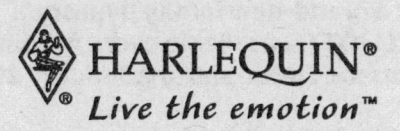

HARLEQUIN®
Live the emotion™

www.eHarlequin.com

Harlequin Blaze

Connect with...The HotWires!

A sizzling new three book miniseries from popular author

Samantha Hunter

Start with Ian's story in
Fascination, on sale December 2005

Then get ready for Sarah's sexy tale in
Friction, on sale January 2006

And finish with E.J.'s finale in
Flirtation, on sale February 2006

The HotWires: this covert team sparks desire...and danger.

Watch out!

www.eHarlequin.com

HBTHW1205

If you enjoyed what you just read,
then we've got an offer you can't resist!

Take 2 bestselling novels FREE!
Plus get a FREE surprise gift!

Clip this page and mail it to MIRA®

IN U.S.A.
3010 Walden Ave.
P.O. Box 1867
Buffalo, N.Y. 14240-1867

IN CANADA
P.O. Box 609
Fort Erie, Ontario
L2A 5X3

YES! Please send me 2 free MIRA® novels and my free surprise gift. After receiving them, if I don't wish to receive anymore, I can return the shipping statement marked cancel. If I don't cancel, I will receive 4 brand-new novels every month, before they're available in stores! In the U.S.A., bill me at the bargain price of $4.99 plus 25¢ shipping and handling per book and applicable sales tax, if any*. In Canada, bill me at the bargain price of $5.49 plus 25¢ shipping and handling per book and applicable taxes**. That's the complete price and a savings of over 20% off the cover prices—what a great deal! I understand that accepting the 2 free books and gift places me under no obligation ever to buy any books. I can always return a shipment and cancel at any time. Even if I never buy another The Best of the Best™ book, the 2 free books and gift are mine to keep forever.

185 MDN DZ7J
385 MDN DZ7K

Name	(PLEASE PRINT)	
Address	Apt.#	
City	State/Prov.	Zip/Postal Code

Not valid to current The Best of the Best™, Mira®, suspense and romance subscribers.

Want to try two free books from another series?
Call 1-800-873-8635 or visit www.morefreebooks.com.

* Terms and prices subject to change without notice. Sales tax applicable in N.Y.
** Canadian residents will be charged applicable provincial taxes and GST.
All orders subject to approval. Offer limited to one per household.
® and ™are registered trademarks owned and used by the trademark owner or its licensee.

BOB04R ©2004 Harlequin Enterprises Limited